THE TOMATOES OF TIME

To Peter

Hope you enjoy.

Rex .

To Erica, for her love and tolerance.
To Nicola and Lois, for just being.

THE TOMATOES OF TIME

The Runford Chronicles
Book two

by
Rex Merchant

Published by

Norman Cottage

Chapter One.

Malcolm Gotobed had deliberately left it until it was dark before he ventured out of the Scouts' hut to go home. That evening was his first time as relief leader to the First Runford Scout Troop and the whole evening had been one long disaster. He locked the door behind him, turned to walk through the dark churchyard and fell over an old iron bedstead, lying across his path.

"Vandals!" He muttered aloud. "That's the last straw! Fancy dumping such rubbish on consecrated ground." It was only then, Malcolm noticed a tall man standing close by the iron framework.

"Oh! Sorry old chap. I wasn't calling you a vandal. I've just fallen over this heap of junk. It wasn't here carlier when my wife dropped me off for the scout meeting."

The stranger leaned forward and peered through the gloom at the tubby scoutmaster. Malcolm cringed under his keen gaze and shrank back into the shadow of the doorway. This was exactly what he had tried to avoid by lingering in the scout hut until the daylight failed. He had fervently hoped no one would see him.

Malcolm had taken over the scout troop that very evening, filling in for the regular leader who was away on holiday. In his enthusiasm he had made the mistake of wearing his old scout uniform. He had taken it proudly out of his wardrobe and removed the mothballs, not realising it was at least forty years out of date.

1

What a sight I must look, he thought, like some latter day incarnation of Baden-Powell, in this bush hat and baggy shorts. One of the lads even suggested I tie corks to my brim and go walkabout in the outback! I was the only one there in short trousers. How am I ever going to face them again?

"Your pardon, I beg." The tall man interrupted his thoughts, speaking with a definite foreign accent. He bowed stiffly from the waist, and clicked his heels. "Some help I need. Please, could you assist me? In England in 1996 am I not? Or are we in South Africa and you are a military scout in the Boer War?"

Malcolm felt himself grow hot with embarrassment. Those sarcastic comments cut him deeply but he forced a smile. A scout was ever helpful, he reminded himself. Perhaps this chap was lost. Maybe the comments were a genuine misunderstanding, for the man was definitely not a local, and there had been no trace of a smile in his voice. Malcolm knew everyone in town and the man's foreign accent sounded mid-European. His bearing reminded the scoutmaster of a Ruritanian officer in one of those stage musicals the Operatic Society produced; with a mixture of stiff upper lip and old-world, military correctness.

"I'm Malcolm Gotobed." He extended his hand. "I'm the town's chemist and a locum scoutmaster; hence the er ... the er ...uniform."

"Ah! That everything explains." The stranger nodded vigorously. "You will help me, I'm sure. A hostelry I need to find, to lodge for the night."

"You'd better walk with me into town. I pass by the Dog in a Doublet on my way home. The landlady, Mrs Lydia Postlethwaite, does a good bed and breakfast, I understand." Malcolm stepped around the iron bedstead to join his new acquaintance and frowned at the offending object.

2

When he looked closer he could see numerous wheels and cogs fitted into the framework.

"What a strange thing that is." He shook his head doubtfully as he pointed to the ironwork. "I thought at first it was a bed frame but now I'm not so sure."

"Definitely a European medieval turret clock, it looks to me," the stranger volunteered.

" Funny place to leave a clock. Perhaps the vicar's expecting it. But it's a peculiar time of day to deliver such a big item. It's a good job it's a fine night; if it rains it might rust the thing."

As they passed under the street light at the entrance to the churchyard, Malcolm noticed the clothes his new acquaintance was wearing. He glanced out of the corner of his eyes at his companion, not wishing to be caught staring hard and giving offence; after all, he himself was not the best dressed man about town, in his tight scout uniform. The stranger's clothes glittered under the light as if they were woven in a metallic thread. The man seemed to be wearing a tinfoil weave, which reflected the light like a polished sheet of aluminium. But strangely, it didn't clank or rustle, and it fitted him as any well tailored suit would.

I do hope we don't meet anyone in town, Malcolm prayed fervently to himself. It's bad enough me wearing baggy shorts and this wide brimmed hat, but he looks like a visitor from the X files. Maybe he's an actor in a Science Fiction film? Heaven forbid my twin brother, Oswald, gets to hear of this! He'd never let me live it down.

"That's the hotel, the Dog in a Doublet." Malcolm stopped in the shadows by a corner garden and pointed beyond a full line of washing to the brightly lit public house. He had no intention of actually setting foot inside the pub, because his twin brother, Oswald, was sure to be propping up the bar.

3

Besides, Malcolm never drank alcohol, except the weekly sip of communion wine and a small medicinal brandy on doctor's orders, when he was at death's door from a heavy cold.

"My thanks to you, Mr Scoutmaster. Most helpful you have been." The man clicked his heels and inclined his head stiffly. He made no move towards the public house but lingered in the shadows by the darkened garden, waiting for his bare kneed companion to waddle off into the night.

Malcolm noticed the hesitation and assumed it was his own appearance that was embarrassing the stranger. He walked a short distance before he realised there had been no telltale crunch of shoes on gravel as the man crossed the Dog in a Doublet car park. The chemist glanced back curiously. There was no one in sight. He turned his head to look closer as he crossed to the darker side of the street, but he could still see no sign of the stranger. Malcolm frowned. This was even more peculiar than the turret clock's sudden appearance. He had heard no movement but his new friend was nowhere to be seen. He hesitated, staring hard towards the pub lights. The only movement he could detect was the shadowy figure of a man in dungarees, removing the dry washing from the garden of the corner house. Shrugging off his curiosity, the scoutmaster slunk into the shadows, hunching his shoulders and bending his head forward to keep the wide hat brim well over his features. Malcolm intended getting home unrecognised.

Chapter Two.

There was always a rush of prescriptions to dispense when Gotobed Bros., Chemist & Druggist, opened for business in the morning. Malcolm Gotobed, known to all the customers as The Chemist, stood at one end of the dispensing bench, making an ointment. His twin brother, Oswald, who was also a pharmacist but insisted on the obsolete title of Druggist, stood at the other end, by the telephone, counting tablets into a bottle.

"Were you at the Dog in a Doublet last night, Oswald?"

"Yes, why?" Oswald bristled, glaring at his brother over his reading glasses, anticipating yet another sermon on the dangers of the demon drink and the importance of sobriety.

"I directed a stranger there. He needed a bed for the night."

Oswald relaxed, deftly wrapped the bottle of tablets and handed them to Roger, the young trainee, who was manning the counter and giving out the completed prescriptions.

"There would be no mistaking him, if you'd seen him. He was a tall military looking chap. He spoke with a European accent."

"Oh, him! An old fellow with grey hair and a goatee beard. Lydia put him in her best room."

"What did you think of that metal suit he was wearing? I've never seen anything like it before."

Oswald stopped dispensing, put down the bottle of tablets he was counting, and raised his eyes in disbelief to the top shelf, where the sparkling antique glass drug bottles advertised an earlier age of pharmaceutical elegance.

"Have you been at the Surgical Spirit? He was certainly dressed oddly but there was nothing metallic about his outfit. Anyway, if my informants are to be believed you're the one who looked a right wally last night."

"What was he wearing then, when you saw him?" Malcolm mumbled, embarrassed by his brother's cutting remarks and trying to ignore the reference to his scout uniform.

"I can remember exactly what he was wearing. I might have been in the pub but I was stone cold sober. It sticks in my memory because Lydia commented about him at the time. You don't often see a man in a crumpled boiler suit under a pink fluffy cardigan; not even in the Dog in a Doublet."

Before Malcolm could protest, Roger put his head around the dispensary screen and interrupted the brothers.

"Can we display these two posters for the flower and vegetable shows, Mr Gotobed?"

"Leave then behind the counter. I'll see to it later." Malcolm let the locals use the noticeboard on the shop side door, to announce forthcoming events. The horticultural shows were regularly advertisers.

"Two posters again? Why don't they combine their two shows and hold one big day instead of two separate events, a fortnight apart?" Oswald asked testily.

6

"You know the Horticultural Society and the Allotment Holders' Association, they're both jealous of their independence, even though most of the members belong to both organisations."

Oswald scowled. He knew the local gardeners liked two bites of the cherry; two chances to win a silver cup and two excuses to get drunk on cheap beer in the members' tents. He stopped counting the tablets, and smiled secretly to himself. Come to think of it, it's high time I renewed both of my subscriptions, he thought. Two shows means I also have two chances of buying cheap booze!

"I'm going to enter my prize tomatoes in one of the shows." Roger interrupted the twins again.

Oswald smiled sarcastically at the lad, much as he would at a child who had just announced he'd found an error in Einstein's Theory of Relativity. With all the expert gardeners locally, with people like Greenfingers Clay, the head gardener at the Hall, entering his produce, Roger stood no chance.

The lad's interest in gardening stemmed from his failure in the A level Botany exam. When he announced he was to study at night school for a resit, Malcolm, in his usual put-the-world-right way, suggested some practical experience in horticulture might increase his chances of success. Observing plants at first hand would help him understand his teacher better.

Oswald never missed a trick. Ever the practical bachelor with an eye to his own needs, he had willingly turned over his entire garden to the eager youngster, giving him the complete run of the greenhouse, the antique lawnmower and all the other rusty tools. His garden had never looked so tidy. Things were certainly growing everywhere. But, Roger producing a prize crop of tomatoes; that had to be a joke!

"Which show will you enter?" Malcolm asked with genuine interest; he liked to be seen showing an interest in the boy.

"It will have to be the first one. I don't think my single tomato plant will produce enough fruit for both shows, and they're very nearly ripe already."

"One single solitary tomato plant!" Oswald scoffed under his breath. "Some hopes you have of beating the allotment holders with their full greenhouses, or Greenfingers Clay with his vast resources. Up at the Hall he has acres of glass, thousands of plants, and decades of show-winning know-how at his fingertips. I could think of a better use for your meagre crop; something like a salad sandwich for my lunch, springs to mind."

As they completed the last prescription of the early rush, the telephone rang. Oswald grabbed it before anyone else could move.

"It's the vicar for you." He pushed the receiver at his brother, disappointed it was not for him. While Malcolm answered the call, Oswald took a small almanac from his pocket and opened up the pages, pretending he wasn't eaves dropping on the telephone conversation.

"Yes, I saw it there as I left the scout hut ... in fact, I fell over the thing." Malcolm told the vicar.

"I assumed you would know all about it, vicar. You left the hall only ten minutes before me. Surely you noticed it there? ... Oh I see! It wasn't there then. Well, I never! ... Then it must have been delivered between you going home and me locking up." Malcolm transferred the receiver to his other ear and began to look decidedly concerned.

"Yes, I suppose you are right vicar ... it would be impossible to back a lorry through the church gateway ... I don't know how it was delivered ...

... I wasn't outside at the time."

Oswald looked at his Almanac, half his mind on Nostradamus and his predictions, the other half on his brother's intriguing conversation.

" ... I know it looked like a bedstead, I thought that myself at first ...Well someone must know what it is... In my opinion, it's a European medieval turret clock." Malcolm trotted out the explanation he had gleaned from the grey-haired stranger; he liked the sound of it and let the words roll off his tongue, adopting it for his own. Perhaps he couldn't tell the vicar how the thing came to be in the churchyard, but at least he knew what it was.

Oswald frowned and put down his book. Malcolm wouldn't know a medieval turret clock if it came into the shop with a prescription. As for telling its nationality! European indeed! Who was he kidding? As soon his brother put down the telephone, Oswald asked him outright.

"What's this about a turret clock?"

"When I left the scout meeting last night, I found someone had delivered a large iron clock to the churchyard. I assumed the vicar knew all about it."

Oswald drew in a deep breath and was about to pour scorn on his brother's knowledge of antique clocks when the trainee brought in a handful of late prescriptions. Abruptly the Druggist sped to the dispensary doorway to escape the extra work.

"Its time for my tea break. I must spend some time planning my lecture to the RUFS." That last remark he shouted over his shoulder as he hurried away from the dispensary, dodged behind the chemist counter, and ran down the cellar steps to his private, basement laboratory.

Malcolm watched his brother's hasty retreat with a pained and disappointed look in his eyes. Oswald and he had been partners in the Runford Pharmacy for some years, but since his brother had become High Wizard to the Runford Union of Fenland Slodgers, he had no time for their business. The RUFS, that South Lincolnshire esoteric society devoted to the study of magic, fortune telling, and other choked-up backwaters of learning, had much to answer for. Now Oswald preferred to study magic spells and prepare his potions down in his cellar workshop.

At college Oswald had excelled at chemistry and had taken an interest in the old Alchemists. Perhaps the seeds had been sown then? It's a wonder he doesn't insist on being called an alchemist instead of the equally obsolete 'Druggist'. Malcolm was proud to have won the Pharmacognosy prize at college. With his interest in medicinal plants he was enjoying coaching the trainee for his Botany exam.

Malcolm stared thoughtfully after his brother. They were so alike physically; both small with curly dark hair, topping their chubby red faces. With maturity they had developed a hint of distinguished grey at the temples and their waistlines had expanded with middle-age prosperity. There the similarity ended. Temperamentally, we are so unalike, Malcolm mused. Not so much chalk and cheese as butter and ground glass!

Sometimes Malcolm had this vivid nightmare about two beans in a pod. They were Euphorbiaceous Sebastiana, Mexican jumping beans. The two identical beans lay side by side in their womblike pod. They both looked healthy and well formed seeds but one was infested with the notorious larva which wriggled and twisted beneath its shiny shell, causing the damaged bean to jump and gyrate like a bean possessed. Oswald was that restless being.

10

He was always agitated, ever ready to jump in feet first, endlessly eager to take the wrong path in life. Wasting his time playing at magic and the like.

Oswald ran back up the cellar steps. "It could be, this turret clock is a gift for the RUFS from Theo Willis, the antique dealer. He promised to present the Union with a clock, to celebrate his appointment to the post of RUFS' librarian."

Oswald hardly gave his brother time to digest this information, before turning on his heels and rushing back down the stairs.

"Hang on one minute, brother. Why do you think the clock in the churchyard could be the one Theo promised you? Why have it delivered to the wrong place?"

Oswald halted in mid flight. "That's easy to understand. Theo lives and runs his shop at Church House, and he has promised to get the RUFS a clock. I suppose the driver simply misread the address. I'll phone Theo after lunch break and tell him it's arrived. He can meet me in the churchyard and we can take a look at it. I must rush now. I've a speech to write and my alembic is boiling over." He threw these last comments over his shoulder as he vanished into his workshop, slamming the door firmly shut behind him.

Malcolm dispensed the last of the prescriptions then took the two posters out into the street to pin them to the side door. He took down an old notice advertising the last church jumble sale and was just replacing it with the first of the horticultural show posters when a tall gentleman sidled up to him. Malcolm instantly recognised the goatee beard and cropped grey hair of his companion from the evening the turret clock arrived. Surprisingly the stranger recognised the chemist, in spite of the lack of khaki shorts and broad brimmed hat.

"For helping me find good lodgings, I thank you. You were correct. Mrs Postlethwait, a good hostelry keeps. Now, tell me, this horticultural show, when will it be?" The man tapped a long forefinger on the newly posted notice.

"On Saturday. It's held in the park. Gates open at ten in the morning."

The stranger nodded his thanks, bowed stiffly and marched off down the street.

"He's not at all the sort of man I would expect to be interested in a local flower and vegetable show," Malcolm muttered, as he fixed up the other poster, advertising the second show, scheduled for two weeks later.

Chapter Three.

Oswald arrived at the churchyard several minutes before Theo Willis. He stood by the scout hut door and muttered uneasily to himself as he eyed the turret clock.

"My God Theo! It's huge! Why did you buy such a damn great thing? I can't see it fitting in the RUFS' library, let alone on the mantelpiece!"

Theo arrived breathless and exhausted. "Ah! ... You've beaten ... me to it." He flopped his considerable weight down on a flat leather seat attached to the clock frame and gasped for breath. "Sorry I was late ... had to view the antiques at the auction rooms ... There's a sale tomorrow."

Oswald ignored the excuses and went straight to the point.

"It's a bit bloody big, isn't it, Theo?"

"Well ... it's a bit bigger than I expected." The librarian admitted defensively. "But, an early turret clock like this will be large and it could be very valuable."

Oswald stalked around the framework, taking in all the details of the clock. The more he inspected its Zodiac decorations, the less at ease he felt. He knew it was usual, in the middle ages when this clock was built, to put the signs for the moon and planets on them. Court Wizards, Astrologers and Alchemists were commonplace in those days. They would undoubtedly have had a hand in such an important project.

Oswald himself, was no stranger to astrology; on those occasions when his post as High Wizard warranted it, he gladly used the ancient art. But this clock gave him the creeps. There was just something about it that didn't ring true.

"What exactly do you mean, Theo. 'Could be extremely valuable'? Surely you know how valuable it is? You purchased it to give to the RUFS, didn't you?"

"Quite so, quite so." Theo agreed hastily. He had indeed rashly promised a clock to the Union, in his first flush of pleasure at being offered the job of librarian. But a battery driven carriage clock costing about £2 was what he had in mind when he made the suggestion. Now his scheming mind was working overtime. Here, out of the blue, was a valuable antique timepiece. It was absolutely free of charge, and people were assuming he had ordered it as a generous gift for the RUFS. It had cost him nothing, because this was the first he had heard of it. And the RUFS would be eternally grateful to him. If, by some happy chance, they didn't want the clock, or they tired of it, he could ask for it back and sell it through his antique shop. From where he sat, it appeared he just couldn't lose.

Oswald continued his inspection noticing a name inscribed on the lower frame. Portius somebody–or–other, it read; he couldn't be bothered to stoop down to decipher it properly. There's nothing unusual in that, he thought, everybody used Latinised names in the middle ages. Even old Nostradamus had done it. But there were aspects of this clock that worried him. It had the appearance of being very old but the finish was far too perfect. It reminded him of one of Theo's fake Lincolnshire Dressers, all stains and polish with false woodworm holes drilled into it and distress marks added with a bicycle chain. Unaccountably the Wizard felt the hairs rising on the back of his neck and a chill crept down his spine. He questioned Theo further.

14

"I understand it's European. Tell me, did you negotiate its purchase from our twin town in Bavaria?"

"Of course, of course. That's precisely what I did," Theo agreed too readily. He stood up, looked around the deserted churchyard and glanced up at the sky. "We should move it indoors. What if it rains? It will ruin the ironwork. Tell me, is there room for it anywhere in the Union?" It was a fine day with no chance of rain but Theo was aware the clock must be moved out of sight in case the real owner turned up to claim it.

Oswald shook his head emphatically. He was a committee member of the RUFS and knew what accommodation they had.

"It's far too big. You should have considered the size of it when you spoke for it."

"Ah well, this is the first time I've actually seen the clock."

Oswald turned and glared at the antique dealer in disbelief.

"I bought it unseen ... on the telephone ... you understand." Having dug himself even deeper into his pit of lies, Theo searched frantically for a quick way of avoiding detection. "Let's call an emergency committee meeting for this afternoon. This needs sorting out urgently."

The extraordinary meeting was called at the churchyard followed by a discussion at the Dog in a Doublet; this latter venue ensured every member turned up. The meeting was impressed with Theo's generosity and his choice of a valuable clock.

"After all," someone commented, "he is an antique dealer and he should know all about these things."

No one else seemed to notice the evil aura that Oswald felt when he approached the mechanism. His was the lone dissenting voice. The other committee members, once they adjourned to the pub for refreshments, even decided on a place to house this gift; there was an unused room in the eaves, above the Union library.

The only problem would be getting the clock up the narrow, spiral, iron staircase into the attic, but Theo hastily suggested they knock out the side window and rebuild the mechanism up there.

"Theo says that clocks of that period are very rare and it will be a good investment."

"It can be seen from the market place and if we put a bell on it they'll hear it all over Runford."

"I don't know of another town in the Lincolnshire fens with such a rare prize."

There seemed a dozen excellent reasons why the RUFS should spend their hard-earned funds on the restoration of this latest acquisition. The High Wizard's lone dissenting voice was overruled. The committee enthusiastically decided to accept the gift and to contact Frank Hogg, the clock restorer, to get the clock moved that very day.

After the meeting, Oswald told his brother. "I've nothing against medieval turret clocks per se, but this one worries me. I can't put my finger on the reason but it gives me the willies! How it got here is a complete mystery. No one saw it being delivered. No one knows how the carrier got it through the church gate. I'm not one bit surprised the burghers of our twin town decided to part with the thing. I'm having nothing to do with it."

Malcolm raised his eyebrows and tutted in sympathy. He had been the first to see the clock and he was intrigued by it. "I've been giving the incident some thought, Oswald. Perhaps that old gentleman, who's lodging with Lydia, can throw some light on the subject. He was standing in the churchyard when I walked out of the scout hut yesterday evening."

"Ah him! Funny you should remind me. He was wandering about the churchyard reading the gravestones, while we were holding our meeting. He seemed very interested in the area. Perhaps he has some ancestors buried here.

16

I'll ask Lydia about him next time I'm in the pub. She'll know his name and it might ring a bell with the vicar."

Chapter Four.

Lydia Postlethwaite was thrilled with her new guest. He was a perfect gentleman of the old school. Always courteous and well mannered; regularly taking the trouble to thank her for looking after him. As an added bonus he never ate at the pub, even though her standard charge included breakfast and an evening meal. She concluded he must have friends in the area, who had invited him to eat with them.

Lydia was standing behind the bar, polishing beer glasses and commiserating with her next door neighbour. "You say some one stole your wife's washing?"

The customer thumped put down his empty glass on the bar. "Took my boiler suit what I wear to work. Took the wife's best pink cardigan, what she had off of me, as an anniversary present. Both things was drying on our washing line in the front garden. Nothing is sacred these days."

"You're so right. I had six pairs of French knickers taken from the back yard only last month. I was lucky though. The vicar's wife returned them to me. She'd found them in her husband's car. Seems he'd picked them up off the road after the thief discarded them... mind you, I still can't fathom how she knew they was mine."

The conversation was interrupted when the new guest strode through the bar and made for the private quarters.

18

"Did you want a mug of cocoa, Mr Butta...daeus? I always make myself one at bedtime." Lydia stumbled on the foreign sounding name, but he had definitely signed himself in as John Buttadaeus, in the guest register.

"Thank you. No, dear lady. To my bed I will go early." The lodger went upstairs to his room, bolting the door firmly behind him.

Lydia busied herself about the bar, content that the old gentleman was probably feeling tired from his travels. After all he had come all the way from the continent; a fact proved by his accent and his foreign sounding name.

Upstairs, in his room, John Buttadeaus did not get ready for bed but swallowed a couple of meal replacement tablets and switched on the television, placing a small, matt black box beside it. In his native language he commanded. "Right, Omni. Remind me of all the data on the vegetable show."

The black box emitted a low squeak and replied.

"Newspaper files for the end of the twentieth century are on screen, master."

"I'm feeling lazy. Read them aloud to me. As they say in this century, why keep a dog and bark yourself."

There was a high pitched sigh from the black box.

John glared at his information robot. "You may posses an artificial IQ of 500; you may well be omniscient; but any more of that and you'll definitely be redundant!"

The box nervously cleared its artificial throat and began to read aloud.

"Lincolnshire Monthly Free News, August 1996. Headline: 'Everlasting Tomatoes.' Report reads: 'New ground was broken this month when the coveted silver cup for the best exhibit in the Runford Horticultural Show was won by a basket of everlasting tomatoes. This new strain was the result of secret genetic engineering. Mr Gotobed, a local chemist and spokesman for the winner, said 'This fruit will never rot.'

19

The press officer for the Runford branch of Feed the Starving, said, 'If this proves to be true, we could feed the starving millions of the third world with them.' No one was available to comment from the Commercial Tomato Growers Association. Shares in ordinary tomato seeds have fallen..."

"Enough! Enough! What about the national newspapers and the scientific journals?"

"Nothing on file, master."

"Instigate a search up to our own time. See if there is any mention of it right up to the day we left home, in the year 2500."

The black box hummed to itself and the TV screen flickered madly as data was retrieved, searched and rejected.

"There is one report of the prolonging of the storage life of fruit for up to six months, and the subsequent processing into meal replacement tablets. That seems to be the state of technology up to our own time."

"You stupid box! Don't you think I know all that already? Don't you forget, I have spent the last twenty years of my existence searching for the secret of eternal life. I've been at it, non-stop, since my 160th birthday. If these twentieth century claims are true, the breakthrough I am seeking was made here in Runford at this exact point in time. Imagine! These primitive fenland idiots had the secret of eternal life at their fingertips over three hundred years before I was even born. And they did nothing with it!"

Omni sighed. It was resigned to its master's ramblings.

The old man smiled and rubbed his hands together with satisfaction. "I have timed my arrival just right. When these wonderful tomatoes win the vegetable show, next week, I will obtain them and be in a position to learn their secret." He clicked his fingers, putting the information robot into its resting mode.

Reclining on his back, practising advanced twenty-sixth century Yoga, John hovered a few inches above the floral duvet.   20

He addressed the empty room. "Those doubters in my own time; I will show them. When I get back with the secret of eternal life, I will apply it..." He caught sight of his own lined face in the dressing table mirror..."Uh! Not before time either!"

Glancing at the silent black box, he continued. "Fancy. One of these morons stumbled on the best-kept secret of nature and didn't recognise the meaning of it. Imagine...everlasting tomatoes. Everlasting means forever. I, John Buttadaeus, will live forever! Think of that. When we have analysed the fruit's DNA, and learned how to apply that secret to my own body cells, I will be immortal; just like the old Gods in the ancient myths and legends"

Chapter Five.

"Oswald...the...turret...clock...it's...
disappeared!" Theo Willis panted as he rushed down the spiral
stairs from the RUFS' attic. He was still spinning, looking like
a prime candidate for a heart attack, when his feet hit the library
floor.

"What do you mean, the clock's disappeared? Frank
Hogg has only just put the damn thing back together. It's a
bloody great big turret clock. We had the window removed to
get the frame up there. How can anything the size of a cast iron,
double bed just vanish into thin air?" Oswald slammed shut the
grimoire he had been consulting and glared at the portly figure
of the Union librarian. He had been expecting trouble with that
clock from the very beginning, but there was little satisfaction
in being proved right; especially when it interrupted his
research.

Theo regained his breath and his face changed from a
dangerous purple to its normal blood red colour. "It just
vanished before my eyes like an apparition. One minute Frank
Hogg and Paddy were fitting the last wheel into the frame, and
the next instant it was not there! Frank vanished, along with
our clock, leaving Paddy and me standing alone in the attic like
a groom and best man deserted at the altar."

"I thought you'd bought a bloody clock movement, not
the Marie Celeste! It can't go swanning off like that; it's not
natural...Anyway, what's Frank's wife going to say? How will
you explain to her, that you've lost him?" Oswald quipped; he
couldn't take the librarian seriously.

22

"As far as Mrs Hogg is concerned, it doesn't matter. She walked out and left him only yesterday. It's the clock that worries me. Come upstairs and see it for yourself; there's nothing there."

Oswald stared up at the library ceiling in disgust, rolling his eyes up under his eyelids. How was he expected to see the damn thing if it had already vanished? He clattered up the iron staircase, closely followed by Theo.

"I told you so. It's gone." Theo said triumphantly.

The Wizard scratched his head. The clock was certainly nowhere to be seen. Paddy Murphy stood alone among the few brick ends left over from the repairs to the window opening. The poor chap looked as bewildered as he did every Saturday night at closing time at the Dog in a Doublet.

"Right then, tell me what's happened, Paddy."

"Jesus! But I was only handing Frank the last wheel, when he just vanished. I didn't do anything wrong. Honest!"

They escorted the dazed Irishman down to the library, where Oswald attempted to question him further. Paddy, shaking with shock, could only repeat what he had already told them. It was only under the Wizard's insistent questioning that the full story came out eventually, in dribs and drabs.

"Big Frank was leaning over the clock frame guiding the escape wheel into its bearings, when there was a sudden whooshing sound. It was like one of them trains leaving an underground station... The clock and Frank just dissolved into thin air."

"How could it?" Oswald couldn't believe his own ears.

"I tell you it did. It was like Theo when it's time for him to pay his round of drinks."

"As quick as that?" Oswald grinned, in spite of his concern for the clock restorer.

"Here, take this fiver from the petty cash, go to the pub and get Lydia to pour you a stiff brandy for your nerves."

Paddy grabbed the note and turned to leave. "I'll be back by tea time. I'll buy some sandwiches and a six pack for Frank and meself." He was showing a touching faith in his friend's safe return.

When they were alone, Theo sat down dejectedly at the library table. "Do you think it's some kind of magic spell? You're supposed to be the expert, Os. What exactly has happened to my valuable clock?"

"You mean some twister in Bavaria has blown his magic dog whistle and the clock has gone back to its master like a faithful German shepherd dog?" Oswald did not conceal his sarcasm.

Theo squirmed in his chair. "Something like that; more or less. Is it possible?"

"Well, there were Zodiac signs all over the damn thing. That's one of the things that put me off it in the first place. Maybe it's bewitched, maybe not." Oswald really hadn't a clue what had happened, but he wasn't going to admit it to the librarian. The loss of the clock was certainly a worry but any damage to his status as High Wizard and local expert on the esoteric would be more painful.

"I'm worried about Frank. Everything he touches seems to be going wrong. He had an accident on his motorbike this morning and his wife has walked out on him." Theo mused.

"All of which is bloody academic as he's vanished into thin air!"

"I know! I know! I was only thinking how disasters have a habit of coming in groups of three."

"Well, you can stop worrying, can't you. Now the poor sod has vanished on your clock, your rule of three is completed." Oswald sarcasm was as acid as raw rhubarb.

24

They sat in silence, each lost in his own thoughts. The only sound, apart from Theo's deepening sighs at the loss of a valuable asset, was the regular tick of the wall clock above the mantelpiece.

Oswald was regretting he had not taken more interest in the ancient timepiece. He had noted the zodiac signs decorating the side rails, and he had even glanced at the Latin inscription on the iron base. It bore the maker's name; Portius somebody-or-other, he recalled. Secretly, he blamed himself for their dilemma. If only he had been more observant, this catastrophe may never have happened. The clock was made in the middle ages. He should have guessed there could be problems; they all dabbled in the occult in those far off days. Now the clock had flown and the evidence was gone, it was impossible to unravel what had happened.

There was a sound like a sudden strong gust of wind above them. Just like a double-decker bus pulling into the depot. Oswald frowned up at the ceiling, the weather forecast had promised a fine, still day.

"Anybody down there?" A wavering voice called from the attic.

"That's Frank!" Oswald stared at Theo in disbelief, before they raced up the spiral staircase.

The restorer was still seated on the leather covered cross-member of the iron frame, leaning forward gripping the escapement rod with both fists. He was hanging on for dear life as if he was griping his motorbike handlebars. His eyes were tightly closed and he wore a shocked expression on his stubbled face.

"Thank God you're back! You and the clock." Oswald was overjoyed at the sight of the man. He breathed a sigh of relief, then paused to take a closer look at Frank, checking lest the experience had affected him in some way.

Oswald was relieved to see Frank was still his ugly self. Still the same hulk of a man with heavy jowls overhanging his double chin and his beer belly bulging in his string vest, which overhung his wide leather belt like an overfilled bag of onions. Frank was almost bald, but sported a pony tail which still hung lankly down his back like one of his own oily, grey, cleaning rags. Several silver earrings dangled from each fat lobe and a dragon tattoo clung to his sweaty neck. Oswald was pleased to see that nothing had changed. Frank Hogg looked perfectly normal for an unsavoury Hell's Angel.

Oswald knew that Frank's scruffy looks were very deceptive for if you allowed yourself to see under the forbidding exterior, the person inside was a gentle, sensitive man. A man who's huge fingers could coax a clapped out clock movement back to health or carve a fine Walnut barley twist column to perfection.

"You feeling alright, Frank?"

"I'm not sure, Mr Gotobed. I just had a funny turn. The room went dim and spun around me." Frank blinked his eyes nervously, eased himself off the clock frame and staggered towards the top of the stairs, feeling his way along the attic wall, hand over hand as if he had vertigo.

Between them they guided him safely down the stairs. Oswald insisted Theo led the way, in case big Frank had another dizzy turn and toppled down the staircase. They sat him in a leather armchair by the open library window and plied him with glasses of water. Eventually he recovered enough to smile thinly and shake his head in bewilderment.

"I'm sorry. What must you think of me? I've never had a strange turn like that before; not even when me motorbike front tyre burst when I was doing the ton on me way home from the pub."

The Wizard smiled reassurance. "Tell me again exactly what happened up there. Don't worry if it doesn't seem to make any sense. I want to hear every little detail."

Frank drained his glass of water and screwed up his stubbled face in concentration. "I was leaning over to take the weight of the escape wheel from Paddy, when I got me vest tangled up in a brass screw. It tore a hole in me vest." He put his hand protectively over the latest tear and rubbed his bruised stomach. Oswald glanced at the torn garment but was unable to tell this new hole from the dozens already there.

"The room revolved around me, just like riding a two stroke on the Wall of Death at the fair. Made me feel bloody sick! ...beg your pardon Mr Gotobed... sorry about the language. "

"I'm sure it would make a saint swear, Frank. Do carry on, It's fascinating."

"Then the attic walls just vanished and I was in Runford churchyard. I saw your brother in the moonlight by the scout hut. I must say, he looked a right wally, dressed in wide army shorts and an Australian bush hat..."

"Is his mind wandering?" Theo stared at the clock restorer in disbelief. "Is he sane?" He whispered hoarsely.

"Shut up Theo! Carry on Frank. This is extremely interesting."

"The churchyard vanished and I was in a strange room...a kind of laboratory. It reminded me of that Frankenstein film I saw on the telly. There was this elderly man dress up in a cooking foil suit; covered him from neck to ankles like he was an oven-ready chicken, it did."

"Did anyone speak to you or show any signs of seeing you?"

"The old fellow jumped onto the seat and pushed me along it. He took some sort of control levers in his hands and we whirled off again until we finished up back here. That's when I shouted down to you." Big Frank relaxed back into the armchair and absentmindedly rubbed his bruised stomach. A low growl of hunger rumbled through the holy vest.

Oswald glanced uneasily at the library ceiling and frowned. "Did this stranger in the metal suit actually come back with you?"

"Only as far as the churchyard. He got off there. I suppose he'd only bought as ticket to that stop." Frank's answer was almost drowned by an even louder rumble from his empty stomach.

"I think you had better get over to the chip shop and have a meal. You can tell me anything else that occurs to you, while we eat. Afterwards we'll come back here and inspect the clock properly. Are you coming with us, Theo?"

"No. My wife is expecting me for lunch, then I will do a bit of clearing up here and go over to the sale room; there's an antique sale on."

As Oswald ushered his companions out of the Union building, there was a creaking sound from the attic. He glanced apprehensively up at the ceiling, hoping the clock was still there, and cursing the effect the thing was having on his nerves.

Chapter Six.

At the fish café, Oswald and Frank sat by the window overlooking the pavement. The owner placed them there as a living advertisement for his meals, as Big Frank always ordered double portions of everything and tucked into his food as if he was due to have his jaws wired together. In contrast to his large companion, Oswald picked at his plate, spearing the mushy peas one at a time on his fork and trying to guide the conversation back to the question of the disappearing turret clock.

"I know it must have been a funny old day for you, Frank. Did I hear you had an accident on your motorbike?"

"S'right, Mr G. Some silly sod on a tractor tore out of a gateway and knocked me off, as I was coming into town. Good thing I had on me crash hat and leathers. I shall have to repair the old girl before I can ride her again."

Oswald nodded sympathetically. It was well known how much Frank Hogg loved his motorbike. He had won several top prizes for the best Harley-Davidson special at the fenland bike shows. In fact some folk said he thought more of it than he did his wife.

"What's this I hear about your wife?"

Frank stabbed viciously at a chip with his knife. "She's gone!" He said abruptly.

"Not for good, I hope."

"We shall have to wait and see, Mr Gotobed. She's upped and taken herself to that Women's Refuge near the railway crossing."

"But she's not a battered wife, surely? You're not the kind of man to be violent. I've always regarded you as the gentlest of giants."

"I haven't lifted a finger to her, but she's gone. Left me for one of her old college lecturers; some woman who was part of the squat at Greenham Common, years ago when they was protesting about nuclear bombs. I don't understand why she's gone. All I can think is, I spend too much time on me motorbike."

"It could be worse. You could drink a lot, like Paddy."

"That's what I said, but she took no notice."

"I'm sure she'll see sense after a night or two away. Things always look better at a distance." Oswald hesitated at this last remark, looked at his companion, who was eating like it was an Olympic event, and thought ungraciously, 'in your case, about ten miles away would be just near enough!' He changed the subject back to what was really bothering him.

"Tell me again. What exactly happened when you had that peculiar turn on the turret clock."

Frank munched his way through two chip dinners, with extra sausages and double mushy peas, helped along with four buttered rolls, while he related his experience. Oswald formed a good idea of what had happened but he kept his conjectures to himself; there was no need to alarm the restorer with such speculations. A far as the Wizard could see, the clock had travelled back in time, going first to Runford churchyard on the evening his brother had played at scoutmasters. The remarks about Malcolm at the scout hut clinched the matter beyond any doubt; not many people were aware of that fiasco or of the silly uniform he had worn. Then Frank had journeyed back to wherever the clock had come from.

30

Oswald's only conclusion was that the clock, with Frank an unwitting passenger, had moved back in time as well as space. Maybe it was some kind of space/time machine? Frank must have accidentally activated the thing when he got the mechanism entangled in his string vest. He probably went back to Europe, where the clock had originated. The shadowy figure, he reported seeing in the laboratory, might well come from that era. He might even be the machine's inventor!

As he watched Frank clean his plate, Oswald thought over the implications of the morning's events. He determined to check the clock over for himself, but he would wait until he could do it alone, in case he was wrong. If he was going to make a fool of himself, he always preferred to do it in private.

"If I were you, Frank, I'd take the rest of today off. You still look pale from your harrowing experience." Oswald lied about the restorer's complexion, for the enormous lunch had fully restored the rosy glow to his companion's cheeks. "Go home and repair your motorbike."

Frank pushed away his empty plate and leaned across the table to reach the few cold chips remaining on Oswald's plate.

"I think I will do just that, after I collect me tools."

Oswald rose to leave. "I must dash back to the pharmacy and help Malcolm with the lunchtime rush. I do hope you manage to sort out your domestic problems."

Frank belched his agreement.

As soon as the lunch hour rush quietened down at the chemist's shop, Oswald left his brother to look after the customers and walked over to the RUFS' library. He had thought of little else while he had been dispensing the prescriptions. He hoped enough time has elapsed for everyone to leave the building, for since Frank Hogg's experience he was dying to inspect the clock closely.

Unfortunately, when he climbed to the attic he found the restorer was still there, working on the clock.

"Oh, you still at it? I thought we agreed you could go home and mend your motorbike?"

"I'm going, but I wanted to get it clear in my mind exactly what had snagged on me vest."

Oswald put aside his irritation and approached the turret clock, realising Frank might supply vital information.

"It was this damn little lever." Frank pointed to a small, polished brass pointer, nestling against the iron framework.

Oswald sat down on the leather seat, leaned over and checked the small projection. It was a handle, about six inches long, and appeared to move against a scale engraved on the side of the clock.

"You say you pushed it as you leaned towards Paddy? Did you pull it back when you found yourself in that strange room?"

"No. I didn't do nothing. But, I'm sure that chap in the metal suit pulled this other lever, on this other side."

Oswald followed Frank's pointing finger. Sure enough, there was a matching brass lever on the opposite side. And that one had its own engraved scale beside it. He noted all this new information but said nothing.

"I'll be off now." The restorer gathered up all his tools and zipped up his bag, but he hesitated at the top of the staircase. "Before I go, Mr Gotobed, I wonder if you can spare me a minute? I want some advice about Gabriella; she's my wife's Greenham Common friend."

Oswald cocked his head to show he was listening.

"I've gotta problem. This friend of Freda's made a pass at me. We was alone in my workshop when she suggested we…er…you know. I didn't take up the offer. No way! I don't fancy her and I think too much of my wife, but since that day things have all gone wrong."

Oswald listened in silence while Frank stumbled through that long speech, then he put on his, serious, professional manner and advised the best he could.

Frank took in the advice, hanging on every word. Finally he left, glad to have unburdened himself to a sympathetic ear. "Tell Mr Willis I'll be back sometime tomorrow to carry on the restoration work."

Oswald watched him go down the iron stairway and listened for him leaving the building. Once he was alone he took a torch from his pocket and checked every inch of the clock movement for himself. The Zodiac signs seemed to be only for decoration; they certainly were not placed in any special sequence to have a magical effect. The Latin name, Portius somebody, turned out to be Portus Temporis.

"Well Portus, old chap, It seems I got your name wrong." Oswald grunted as he moved on to examine the clock wheels. Under a coat of rust coloured paint, the wheels looked brand new; there was no sign of wear. "Hardly the state one would expect a medieval turret clock to be in." Suddenly a disturbing thought struck him.

"Damn me! Portus Temporis, the Gateway of Time! My Latin must be getting very rusty for me to have missed that simple phrase."

Oswald was convinced more than ever that the iron framework was nothing but a time machine in turret clock's clothing! The rust paint was just a clever attempt to disguise the true age of the mechanism. It was tempting to believe the brass levers would control the machine, making it travel back through time, and Frank had accidentally activated it when he had leaned against it.

The Wizard inspected the right hand lever more closely. The scale bore the Latin word 'Tempus' engraved on it, confirming his suspicions. The other lever bore the word 'Locus'. He searched his memory for remnants of schoolboy Latin and came up with the translation. Locus meant Place!

"Good God! I was right! This machine can be used for time and space travel."

On even closer inspection, Oswald found the time scale was calibrated from zero.

"Could that nought represent the present and the calibrations stretch back into the past? On the other hand, maybe it was meant to go forward!" There were no numbers on the scale. That would make it a chancy business if he tried a little experiment. Frank had gone off into the blue and managed to get back to the present time.

"Maybe that was pure luck; perhaps just one chance in a million?"

The Wizard sat on the leather seat and fingered the brass Time lever. He was dying to activate the machine but wary of being trapped in the dark ages. He sat and pondered his options, getting more agitated and frustrated by the second. It was in his nature to jump first and ask questions afterwards. Finally his impatience got the better of him.

"To hell with caution! Live dangerously, I say. I might as well be Malcolm, if I funk this chance...just one tiny twitch of one lever." He flicked the Time switch on and immediately off again.

Chapter Seven

Theo Willis always attended the local antique sales. He bought old furniture and objets d'art, if they were going for a song. He even arrived at the very beginning, when the rubbish was offered for sale. Rarely did anything worthwhile come up at this early stage, but he couldn't miss the slimmest chance of a bargain.

The antique dealer stood at the back of the hall, chatting to a few of his trade cronies. It was at this stage on sale day, the Ring discussed plans to keep the prices down, by not bidding against each other. There was always some bargaining between dealers about who would bid for what.

The 'smalls' were hotly contested by the ladies seated in the front row. These dealers ran bricabrac stalls at village halls and stood the antique fairs and car boot sales. They sat perched on the edge of their chairs like so many Vultures around a carcass, watching the auctioneer and each other with unblinking eyes, waiting impatiently for each item to be offered, so they could pounce on it. Bidding was rapid but prices were low. Most things sold for a few pounds. It was possible to fill a van for a tenner from the first fifty lots.

Theo was chatting noisily to his neighbour when the auctioneer's voice took on an urgent note. This change in tone alerted the dealer to the fact that something unusual was happening in the hall.

"I have a bid of five thousand pounds." The room went deathly silent. The auctioneer appeared pink and ruffled.

"What was that? How much did he say?" Theo nudged the woman standing in front of him. A dozen hostile eyes turned towards the back of the room. "Hush!" Hissed from a score of pursed lips.

"Are you bidding, Mr Willis?" The auctioneer asked blandly.

"No...no." Theo blustered. "What exactly are you selling?"

"Please pay attention, man. It's lot 25, the oil painting."

Theo gulped in astonishment as the porter held aloft a small, yellow oil painting. The very painting an old lady had offered to sell him in his shop only days before. There must be some mistake. That daub wasn't worth twenty pounds let alone thousands!

"The bidding is on my right. Six thousand pounds...Seven thousand...Eight thousand...Ten thousand..."

Every head swung from side to side as two well-dressed male bidders fought it out from opposing sides of the hall. It was exactly like Wimbledon at the Men's Singles finals.

"Who the hell are they?" Theo whispered.

"Search me. They're not locals. I've never set eyes on either of 'em before."

The auctioneer's voice rose by several octaves as the seesaw battle for the small painting continued. "Twenty thousand...Fifty thousand...One hundred thousand..."

One of the older ladies in the front row, fainted from the tension, but everyone ignored her. Theo choked at the back of the hall. He had refused to part with fifty quid for that very painting. When the old lady walked into his shop with it under her arm and offered it to him for a pittance, he had told her it was worthless. In fact it had been his suggestion, she take it to the sale room where she might get a tenner for it on a good day with the light behind it. Surely these bidders must be wrong. It couldn't be worth so much, could it?

Nothing had ever reached so high a price before at the Runford saleroom

The trouble was, two well-dressed men, with an air of expertise about them, were hammering away at each other with ever increasing bids. One might have made a mistake, but two of them? He began to experience a sick, sinking feeling in the pit of his ample stomach. Perhaps he'd made a mistake, dismissing the painting so flippantly. Maybe he'd missed the bargain of his lifetime!

"Five hundred thousand pounds...Six hundred thousand..." The auctioneer's voice cracked with the tension. He reached over, grabbed the carnations from the vase decorating his rostrum, and drained the cloudy water in one gulp.

"Seven hundred thousand..."

"Make it a round million." One of the bidders suggested in a cultured voice. The room stopped dead. Never before had the magic word, 'million', been spoken within those walls; except in jest. But this was for real! The lady who had fainted, stood up and turned her hearing aid to top volume; its high pitched whistle filled the room.

"Can you repeat that figure, please young man," she shouted above her own feedback.

"I bid one million pounds for that oil painting."

The auctioneer turned his fevered gaze on the underbidder, who was frantically stabbing at his mobile phone, gesticulating madly and signalling for a few minutes respite.

Theo stood on tiptoe to see above the seething mass of people; most of the onlookers were on their feet by then. The rival bidder shook his head sadly, closed his mobile phone and pushed it into the depths of his coat pocket. Dejectedly he rose from his chair and stalked out of the saleroom, shoulders hunched, eyes on the ground, like a man who had just bet his all on the favourite only to see it fall at the last fence.

The crowd parted to let him through, drawing back as if he had some contagious disease.

"Good God!" Theo looked at his neighbour in disbelief. "A cool million spent on one small oil painting, in just five short minutes. Bloody amazing! I wouldn't have believed it. If I hadn't been here."

The room seethed with speculation. Several lady dealers from the front row, rushed up to shake the buyer's hand, as he struggled to pass his business card to the auctioneer. Theo wasn't sure if they fancied the man or they expected his luck to rub off on them. Four burly porters carried the painting out to the back room; it wasn't very heavy, but they were suddenly very security conscious, and they all wanted to touch the item for luck, like superstitious pilgrims at a saint's reliquary. A story like that would be worth innumerable free pints at the pub for weeks to come. The auctioneer mopped his brow with a silk handkerchief and declared an early break for afternoon tea. He rushed off to his office to find his heart tablets and calculate his commission.

In the general melee, as people queued for refreshments at the mobile burger van in the yard, Theo noticed the million pound man slip quietly away. The Runford dealer was bursting with questions about that oil painting, so he followed the departing figure, hoping to speak with him. The man went into the nearest pub, closely followed by Theo Willis.

Lydia smiled at her new customer and pulled him half of bitter.

"I'll get that, Lydia. And I'll have the same." Theo waved a twentypound note at the landlady and beamed disarmingly at the man.

"Thank you, Mr...er...?"

"Willis, Theo Willis. Antique dealer."

The man smiled knowingly but remembering his manners, he directed his benefactor towards a table in the far corner.

"Well, Mr Willis…?"

"Call me Theo, please dear man."

"Well Theo. I guess this is not some chance social encounter. You saw me buy that painting at the saleroom, didn't you? What can I do for you?"

"That is the first million pound ever spent at Runford auctions. That painting must be very special."

"You might say that."

"Please explain, Mr…er…"

"Simon Smith. Buyer for the London Museum of Modern Painters." He handed Theo his business card.

"And who was that painting by? Pablo Picasso or someone equally unlikely?" Theo joked.

"Yes, exactly. Pablo Picasso in his yellow period."

Theo choked on his bitter.

"Did you have a chance to view the painting, Theo? It was signed with a monogram, 'P.P.' Pablo Picasso."

Theo coughed again, violently. He had indeed seen the letters P.P. on the canvas when the old lady handed it to him. He had made a sarcastic comment about some idiot signing it on behalf of somebody else!

Simon Smith carried on explaining. "It's a little-known fact that Picasso had many different coloured periods to his work. Everyone has heard about his famous Blue period, but in my latest book, The Rainbow Painter, I have postulated, red, orange, yellow, green indigo and violet periods, as well."

Theo stared into his glass in disbelief. "I've never heard of anything but his Blue period, and I've been dealing in antiques for years."

"Until today, it was only my hunch, but that nude painting of his mistress, done in his Yellow Period, proves my theory beyond doubt. It also means that painting is worth at least twice what I paid for it." Simon Smith rose from his seat, lifted his business card from Theo's numb fingers and picked up his empty glass.

"Now I must dash. I must arrange shipment of that Picasso, then I have an appointment with the New York Metropolitan Museum."

Theo Willis cried into the dregs of his beer. His ample frame rose and fell spasmodically as he sobbed. "Two bloody million pounds...sniff. Only worth two million...sniffle. Two damned million... Just two million pounds, and I had it in my grasp for a poultry fifty!"

Chapter Eight

There was a swishing sound in Oswald's ears as he sat on the turret clock in the RUFS' attic. He had clicked the Time lever forward and immediately pulled it back again. Momentarily he felt quite dizzy as a sound resembling water rushing down a plughole echoed inside his head. He clung onto the clock frame, waiting for the attic walls to stop vibrating and come back into focus.

Once the room stopped moving, Oswald was amazed to see Frank was there once again. The restorer was gathering up his tools, and putting them into his bag, just as he had a few minutes earlier.

"I'll go now." Frank zipped up his bag once more and repeated word for word, the remarks he had made earlier. "Before I go, Mr Gotobed, I wonder if you can spare me a minute. I want some advice about Gabriella; she's my wife's Greenham Common friend."

Oswald had an attack of deja vue, on top of the vertigo he was suffering, but he kept this knowledge to himself and was careful to offer the same advice to Frank, as he had given the first time. It wouldn't do for Frank to be in two minds about what to do!

"Tell Mr Willis I'll be back some time tomorrow to carry on the restoration work." Frank departed just as he had before.

Oswald snatched his hand away from the brass lever as if it was alive with high voltage. He held his breath until he heard Frank leave the building, then he let out a long low whistle of relief.

"Phew! That was a close call! I wont do that again in a hurry. I might finish up lost in the past. I'd better search the library for books on the relevant magic before I tamper with this thing again." He rose shakily from the seat on the clock frame and ran his fingers gingerly over the Tempus scale. "I'd better make a detailed sketch of these scales so I can study them at my leisure."

Oswald spent the rest of that day in the RUFS' library, researching into Time Magic, searching the grimoires for any clues to understanding the workings of the suspect clock.

Gradually he grew more confident and even succeeding in making the wall clock run backwards. When he tried to send his teatime snack back into its past, the individual fruit pie reverted to its ingredients; a pile of apple pieces, a knob of butter, an egg and a handful of flour. Feeling a bit peckish, he made the necessary passes over the items to return them to their cooked state, but he was to be disappointed. The fruit turned mildew and the egg smelled rancid.

"Just strengthens my theory." He muttered. "Gotobed's Law of Inevitability. The ideal subject for the annual lecture I'm giving to the RUFS on Founder's Day."

Oswald had stumbled on a disturbing fact about some of his magic. Many of the things he altered with his spells seemed to revert back and correct themselves. Last summer, when he had concentrated on Weather Magic, ensuring weeks of fine weather to clear the shop shelves of suntan oils and he had conjured up beautiful fine days for the town's fete and gala, the autumn had been exceptionally wet. Rainfall figures for the year as a whole had still worked out as average for South Lincolnshire. Somehow Mother Nature had redressed the balance. Hence, his musing about his Law of Inevitability.

Oswald put his thumbs in his lapels and pretended to be a barrister.

"Me Lud. If we are destined to be unable to alter things permanently by Magic, then I, Oswald Gotobed, High Wizard to the RUFS, will go down in history as the wizard who postulated the law which explains this phenomenon."

Theo Willis crept into the library, intent on finding an art book to check on oil painters. He was surprised to find the Wizard there, talking to himself, strutting up and down and grasping his jacket collar like a ham actor in a courtroom drama. Theo glanced curiously at the selection of books on Time Magic, spread over the table.

"Doing a bit of research, Os?"

The Wizard wiped the remains of his rancid fruit pie off the table and hurriedly threw it into the bin. Trying to look casual, he sprayed an air-freshener can about the library to hide the sulphurous smell.

"I remember chemistry was called 'stinks', when we were at school, but I didn't realise your magic spells came into the same category." Theo turned his nose up in disgust.

"Absolutely nothing to do with me." Oswald said emphatically, gathering up all his books, hoping to hide the subject of his researches from the antique dealer's prying eyes. In his hurry to avoid Theo's questions, he slammed shut one large volume, accidentally leaving his notes on the two brass levers, trapped between the pages like a bookmark.

"I'll give you a hand to put that lot back on the shelves. After all, it is part of my duties as librarian to keep the place tidy." Theo took some of the heavy volumes and placed them in their correct places on the walls.

"I've just had some damn bad luck." The librarian confided in Oswald as they carried the books from table to shelves. "I was at the antique sale when an oil painting came up for auction. I reckoned it was worth about twenty pounds, but it made a million!

43

Fancy; the sum of one million pounds bid at one of our local sales. I still can't believe it."

"Who the devil paid that sort of lottery money for a painting?" Oswald was not at all interested in art but he was fascinated by huge sums of money.

"One of the country's top art experts, would you believe? The man is a buyer for a national museum collection. And he says the painting is worth double that amount, subject to x-ray confirmation, of course. But that's just a formality."

"How come you didn't spot this bargain? You never mentioned to me there would be a rarity coming up for sale. And, how come you describe this sale as 'your bad luck'? They were your very words."

"You can't know everything in my trade. It was by Picasso, from a little known period of his work. That's why I've come to look him up in the library. Just in case lightning strikes twice and I'm fortunate enough to be offered another of his paintings."

"So you were offered this one, then?"

Theo looked sheepishly at the Wizard, coloured up red and coughed nervously.

"Come on Theo. You said yourself, you can't know everything in your trade."

"I was offered the painting before the sale. The old lady, who owned it, brought it into my shop wrapped up in brown paper. She wanted fifty quid for it. I told her it wasn't worth that much and advised her to take it to the saleroom."

"Oh dear!" Oswald hid his grin with his hand and chuckled silently to himself. "I must be off now. Malcolm will need some help." He lied to excuse himself, hoping to get well away from the librarian before he broke into uncontrollable laughter.

Theo went to the bookshelves to search for works on modern painters. He paused at the Magic section and thoughtfully eyed the selection of volumes on Time Magic that Oswald had been reading.

"What was the old devil up to? Why this sudden interest in time? " He slid one volume partly from the shelf and immediately noticed a slip of notepaper sticking out of it. Theo took the book down from its place and extracted the Wizard's notes. There in the Wizard's handwriting, was an annotated sketch of the Time and Place levers from the turret clock and alongside the drawing, details of how each might work. Theo scratched his head and took the notes from their hiding place to study them properly.

Oswald crossed the High Street and went into the pharmacy, intending to go down to his cellar workshop to write his thesis on the Law of Inevitability, but Malcolm was blocking his way, standing behind the counter, setting up a display of Pig Powders and Cattle Drenches.

"I've decided to lecture the RUFS on Gotobed's Law of Inevitability." The Druggist told his brother, striving to sound important.

"Sounds interesting." Malcolm always made an effort to say the right thing.

With that crumb of encouragement, Oswald really got into his stride, grasping the opportunity to rehearse his arguments.

"You remember last summer, when I ensured months of good weather so that we cleared the overstock of suntan preparations? Well, I was surprised to find we still had the average amount of rainfall that year. I must admit, I was intrigued to discover nature had somehow redressed the balance. It seems inevitable that things will always even out, in the long run.

Hence Gotobed's Law of Inevitability. What do you think of my stupendous discovery? Don't you think people will look back in centuries to come and say what a clever man I was?"

"They might think the Gotobed name refers to me." Malcolm observed playfully,

"Ah! Did I say Gotobed's Law?   I meant Oswald Gotobed's law, of course."

Are you certain it always holds true? After all, you don't appear to have given much thought to the exceptions."

"Perhaps Oswald Gotobed's Rule of Inevitability might sound better as a temporary title." Oswald muttered in a crestfallen voice.

Malcolm paused in his work and smiled at his brother disarmingly.

"Do you remember when we were at school and studied Physics? What was that third Law of Motion that Isaac Newton postulated? Something about every action having an equal and opposite reaction, wasn't it? Your new rule sounds awfully like one of old Isaac's old ones, reworded to sound new; don't you think?"

"Newton wasn't thinking about magic when he made up his law." Oswald said grumpily.

"I wouldn't be too sure about that. Surely Sir Isaac Newton was keen on Alchemy and numerology? He believed in much of the rubbish you talk about. Mind you, that was way back in the 17th century. I suppose there was some excuse for it in those days."

Oswald stomped angrily down the stairs to his cellar workshop and slammed the door so hard, the packets of Pig Powders jumped off the shelf. Malcolm smiled philosophically as he gathered up the fallen stock. It was a small price to pay to get his own back on his cocky brother, for once.

46

Chapter Nine.

Big Frank Hogg sat in his workshop surrounded by swinging pendulums and ticking clocks. He was working on his damaged motorbike petrol tank, pushing out the dents and filling in the hollows and scratches. A Black Forest cuckoo clock wheezed a dull note from its split bellows and broke the biker's concentration. He looked up at the clock, caught sight of a photograph of his missing wife, hanging beside it, and burst into tears again.

"Oh Freda!" He threw down his tools and buried his head in his hands, hiding the swollen cheeks and red rimmed eyes.

"Why did you have to go and run off to that there women's refuge?" He blew his nose on an oily rag and pulled her tear-stained farewell note from his trouser pocket. He read it aloud for the thousandth time that day.

"Goodbye, Frank. You shouldn't have done it to my best friend. Gabriella has told me all about it. I am pissed off with you. Don't try and find us. We are at the women's refuge near the railway crossing."

Frank sniffled and wiped a dew drop from the end of his nose. The cuckoo clock prepared to announce twelve o'clock, mid day. Frank stopped the bird in mid cuck with a well-aimed tin of metal polish. Instantly he regretted his action. He bent the bird back into shape, gently caressed the broken wing with his huge fingers and stuck it back together with a sticking plaster.

47

"What does she mean, 'Gabriella has told me all about it'? Told her all about what? That bloody woman's been nothing but trouble since she came. She might have been a friend to Freda, in her younger days at college, but she ain't no friend of mine!"

Frank thought back to the day Gabriella had arrived on their doorstep. It was only a month ago but it seemed years. Freda and he had never exchanged a cross word until that bloody woman arrived. She was a raving feminist and since that awful day, he hadn't had one proper meal. Freda was a Cordon Bleue cook; she had studied at the Women's Institute, but Gabriella fancied herself as an author. She was writing a cookbook and needed to try out her recipes.

"What sane person would buy The Greenham Common Protestors' Cookbook?" Frank asked aloud. Most of the dishes were invented when the women protestors were living rough in tents, alongside the beleaguered nuclear base.

"Baked Beans and vegetarian sausages, Hedgehog steaks, dandelion leaf tea made with rain water; I bet that's all they ate. And that would be cooked over a smoky camp fire! I'll be pleased when all this culinary research is over."

To further complicate matters, Gabriella had taken a definite fancy to Big Frank. One day, when Freda was at her weekly meditation class in the church hall, Gabriella had waylaid Frank in his workshop. She had stripped off all her clothes and asked him to ravage her. The scene was etched on his mind. Gabby, as his wife liked to call her, threw herself across his workbench, scattering screws and brass, clock bushes in all directions. With her legs outstretched, she demanded satisfaction. She looked like an old hen, with her scraggy buttocks, skinny legs and protruding shoulder blades. Why would he fancy an old boiler like her when he had Freda as a partner? Being a harmless sort of bloke, he had tried to let her down lightly. Summoning up all his sensitivity he had told her.

48

"Put your knickers back on and try the Salvation Army Hostel in Runford; there must be a lot of desperate men in there."

Gabriella dressed in silence and had never mentioned the incident again.

"In fact, come to think of it, she ain't said a single word to me since."

Frank remembered his conversation with Oswald Gotobed, about his problems. The Druggist had suggested something about a 'woman's corns'!

"God! She must have bad feet to go and do a daft thing like that!" It was all beyond him.

"I'm desperate. I need some money and me lottery numbers have missed out again. I'd even sell me motorbike to raise some readies to take Freda away on holiday. I'm sure if we could get away, just me and her, she'd forgive me; whatever it is I'm supposed to have done." The Hells Angel grumbled aloud, then realising what he'd said, he looked apologetically at his damaged motorbike, stood forlornly in the corner of the workshop.

"Well perhaps I'd just pawn you, temporary like, and retrieve you when I got back. I'd make the pawnbroker promise to look after you well."

Frank folded the grubby leaving note, kissed it sentimentally, and pushed it back into the greasy depths of his pocket. He returned to planishing his petrol tank, keen to get his bike back on the road. If he intended visiting Freda at the refuge in Runford, he would need his wheels; besides, he still had some work to do on that peculiar turret clock for the RUFS.

As he polished the yellow lacquer on his restored tank, bringing the new patches up to the high gloss of the original, he thought about that medieval clock. An amazing piece of engineering that was. Apart from the unusual brass levers on the side, the movement was the standard layout for the period. But it showed no signs of wear!

49

Imagine, built in the dark ages, probably six centuries ago like the one in Salisbury cathedral, and the wheels and pinions were still pristine. Even if the clock had never been used since the day it was made, some rust and tarnishing would have set in.

Frank had checked all the metal bearings, even tried to file one of them where there was a slight burr, but his best, modern, hardened steel files wouldn't leave a mark on the clock. The metal was so hard; unusually so, for samples of old iron were normally soft and porous. That clock was a mystery. It crossed his mind, it could be made of an alloy he had never met before.

"What a shame I had that funny turn. Still, it ain't happened since. Must have been worry over my Freda." He would carry on with the work of setting the turret clock up when he'd finished the motorbike. There was no hurry now it was safely set up in the RUFS' attic and out of the weather. Theo Willis had been most insistent he hurried up the work, but then he was probably only worried about thieves and leaving the thing out in the open. It wasn't likely to be stolen from the confines of the library attic.

"I'll ring him when I've had my lunch. I'll explain the delay. He'll understand." Frank addressed this remark to the limp cuckoo as he balanced it on his little finger like a tame wren on a vegetable marrow.

Chapter Ten.

Frank Hogg's telephone rang in his workshop. He thrust the daily paper, he was reading, into his back pocket and jumped up from the workbench, spilling beer and scattering clock parts, in his haste to get to the phone. Maybe Freda was ringing to make things up with him. Perhaps she was on her way home and he could have a proper home-cooked meal.

"Oh! It's you, Mr Willis." Disappointment coloured his voice. "Well...I wasn't planning on coming into town today. I suppose, if it's so urgent I could meet you at the RUFS in an hour."

Frank put down the phone and packed up his tools. Theo had insisted he get to town immediately; it was something to do with the turret clock. The restorer grumbled to himself but his good nature prevailed, and he set out to walk the five miles into Runford, hoping to thumb a lift on the way.

Theo was pacing the RUFS library floor like an expectant father whose first child was a week late. He had read and reread the Wizard's notes, he had found in the magic book. He puffed and tutted to himself as he considered the possibilities in his artful mind. Time travel was a concept he would normally have dismissed out of hand. It was the stuff of science fiction and not to be taken seriously by level headed antique dealers. But, Oswald Gotobed was High Wizard of the RUFS and he obviously believed in it enough to make copious notes about the possibility.

51

There was also Frank's unexplained behaviour when the clock had vanished from the attic.

Frank stomped up to the library, his tool bag tucked under his arm, his size twelve Doc Martens rattling the stair treads. He was met on the top step, by Theo, in a very agitated mood.

"About time! You took your time getting here."

"I ain't got me motorbike now, Mr Willis. You remember I had an accident on it. I walked half way here, then managed to thumb a lift on a farm cart. I've come as fast as I could."

Theo hurried his helper inside and gazed furtively out of the window, checking no one was going to disturb them. He quickly ushered Frank up the spiral stairway to the attic room above the library.

"Did you want the clock in ticking order, Mr Willis?"

"No, not exactly...well, yes...I suppose we do need it working, eventually. But first I want your expert opinion on something more important."

Big Frank beamed. His chest expanded with pride, temporarily pulling in the overhang of his stomach. It wasn't too often, someone as important as Theo Willis, antique dealer and RUFS librarian, asked his humble opinion.

"There are two brass levers on that clock frame that rather baffle me." Theo lied, for he had read Oswald's notes and knew as much as the Wizard himself about them.

"Ah! You mean them ones that caught in me string vest."

"Yes, exactly. I knew you would understand."

Frank beamed again. He didn't understand at all, but it was nice to be complimented anyway. With the loss of Freda, his ego certainly needed bolstering.

"Come over here. You see this Latin writing on the clock frame. Look; here it says Tempus, that means time. On this other side it says Locus; that means place."

52

"I thought it was only doctors, chemists and Romans that knew about Latin. You are the clever one, Mr Willis."

"Quite so, Frank. Now, how can I put this? I think this clock is some kind of Time Machine. I think, you travelled back in time when you had that funny turn." Theo came straight out with the truth, for once. He had toyed with the idea of lying to the restorer, but the more he considered it, the more he realised Frank would need to understand most of what he was doing, if the plan was to succeed. Anyway, Theo consoled himself, the big idiot was a simple fellow and easily led.

"I'm pleased you told me that, Mr Willis. I've never had a funny turn before and it worried me. I can tell you, it's a relief to be told there's nothing wrong with me."

"We need to try an experiment, Frank, my dear fellow. With your help, we can prove this is a real Time Machine. What we need is some sort of irrefutable proof. Something you could bring back from the past as a sign you've actually been there."

Frank looked suitably puzzled. Then a wide smile crossed his face. "What about the arrow what struck 'arold in the eye at the battle of 'astings?"

Theo paused, thought of several sarcastic comments then rejected them all. Normally he would have revelled in his wit but he knew he must not squash the man's enthusiasm and kill the goose that was about to lay his golden egg.

"I don't think we need go to those lengths; it might be dangerous going onto a battlefield...brilliant as your idea is. No. We need only go back a day or two and we needn't travel out of Runford. "

"Needn't we?"

"Well not exactly 'we', you understand. Just you alone are going to try this experiment. I must stay here in case the...er...the telephone rings. Your suggestion about King Harold has given me a brilliant idea. Five days ago, a lady came into my shop at opening time.

53

She offered me an oil painting. I didn't buy it because it wasn't valuable, but she has been on my conscience ever since. Perhaps she needed the money for a sick husband or starving grandchildren. I do so wish I'd helped her out."

Frank nodded sympathetically. It was just the sort of thing that would have worried him.

"I think you could go back in time to that very morning, catch her as she leaves my shop and buy the painting off her for £50. She will be happy with that. I know, and she will be non the wiser it was me that had helped her out. I like to be an anonymous benefactor. That would be conclusive proof." Theo held out a crisp fifty-pound note.

"What a lovely thought, Mr Willis. Shall I dump this worthless painting, once I've bought it?"

"Good God, no!" The dealer panicked at the very thought. "We must have it back here to prove you actually bought it in the past. We need solid proof. Is that understood?"

Frank nodded.

"Right. Take my wristwatch so that you can keep track of how far you go into the past. I've been reading up Einstein's theories, and I'm positive the watch hands will spin backwards and the date numerals will go into reverse, once you start to travel backwards in time."

Frank strapped the expensive watch around his muscular wrist, managing to secure the buckle in the very last hole. He mounted the clock frame, sat on the leather seat, and took the Tempus lever between his huge fingers.

"Ease it back gently. Keep an eye on my watch." Theo crossed his fingers behind his back and watched as the restorer moved the brass lever. Frank eased it along with the infinite care he would have lavished on turning a watch balance staff. There was a sound like air escaping from a huge bicycle pump. The clock, complete with passenger, dissolved into thin air, before Theo's amazed eyes.

54

The librarian gulped in astonishment. He hadn't really dared to believe the thing would work. But it had! He jumped around the attic like a schoolboy on a bouncy castle. All he had to do now was wait for Big Frank to return from the past with his million pound painting.

Chapter Eleven.

Frank Hogg saw the attic walls revolve about him. He checked the wristwatch as the hands spun backwards and the date went into reverse. This time he felt he was in full control of the situation and he actually enjoyed the exhilarating feeling. It reminded him of the first time he did the ton along the top of the sea bank, helmetless on his Harley-Davidson, his pigtail trailing out behind him in the hundred miles an hour slipstream. His adrenaline flowed freely; he felt alive.

Theo, who was standing anxiously by his side, disappeared. The portly dealer dissolved like steam hanging in the air and Frank found himself alone in the RUFS building. That was a bonus in itself. He chuckled, for there was something about the oily antique dealer that he was beginning to dislike. Frank Hogg could sometimes be very perceptive. He dismounted from the clock frame, swinging his leg over the cross member, just as he did on his motorbike, and made his way downstairs to Runford High Street.

Everything outside seemed perfectly normal. People passed the time of day with him, exactly as they usually did. This surprised him at first as he had the notion he would be invisible. Pensioners walked their dogs, paperboys delivered their empty bags back to the newsagents, and children dragged their unwilling feet towards the school. The lollypop lady stopped the traffic for him to cross the busy street as he ambled towards Church House Antiques where Theo Willis had his business

Frank arrived a few minutes early that morning. Mrs Dora Willis was still tidying the shop before opening time. She leaned into the window and placed a small card in the front, advertising a furnished cottage available for holiday rental, then she came to the front door and stepped out into the High Street to sweep the step. Clouds of dust rose into the morning air as she briskly attacked the doormat.

"Morning, Mrs Willis." Frank greeted her cheerfully and leaned against the corner of the building to wait for the lady with the painting. Theo's crumpled fifty-pound note was clutched firmly in his large fist.

Theo's wife eyed the big man suspiciously. It was worrying to find an enormous Hell's Angel, decorated with tattoos, sporting numerous earrings and wearing size twelve boots, loitering outside the shop, first thing in the day. She gripped the broom handle firmly, trying to remember the moves taught at the WI self-defence classes that winter, and the advice given on her favourite Police Watch program.

Luckily, Theo came to the shop door, propped it open with a highly priced, reproduction, cast iron doorstop and picked up his letters from the side table. Frank gave him a little, conspiratorial wave and a broad, knowing wink. The antique dealer smiled back uncertainly, then recognising the big man, sauntered over the doorstep and went over to him.

"What are you doing in town so early, Frank? Come to sort out the church clock again?"

Dora Willis, relieved that her husband knew this suspicious character, went through the shop to the kitchen, to start the household chores.

"I'm waiting for a lady to bring me a valuable oil painting." Frank winked again in a very obvious manner.

"Aren't we all!" Theo raised his eyebrows. He had always regarded the clock restorer as a simple fellow, but now he revised this estimate to something approaching fifty pence short of a pound.

Frank put his hand up to his mouth as realisation hit him. Of course, he had arrived five days before he had set out! He was here and yet he really couldn't be. The antique dealer hadn't yet met the old lady. Did this mean he could meet himself coming back, or maybe bump into himself leaving the newsagents? He sidled off down the path, trying to come to terms with his novel circumstances and sat down on the wooden bench in front of the British Legion. From there he had a clear view of the antique shop. While he was waiting, he took the newspaper from his back pocket and read the news.

Just after nine o'clock, a white haired lady passed by. She was carrying a brown-paper parcel under her right arm. Frank peered after her. He was certain he noticed the edge of a gold picture frame peeping from one corner of the package. She went into the antique shop. Frank could see her talking to the antique dealer, through the window. He sat and patiently waited. If Theo had briefed him correctly the old girl would soon come out of the shop, still carrying her painting.

Minutes later she left the shop, dragging her feet as she walked, her expression disappointed and crestfallen. Frank waited until she was level with him then made a point of wishing her good morning.

"Is it?" She answered gloomily.

"Of course it is, my dear. It's surprising how things can turn out alright; if you only believe they will."

She hesitated, then sat down heavily beside him and propped the framed canvas up against the bench seat.

"Nice looking oil paining, that." Frank ventured.

"That's what I thought. My hubby picked it up in Paris during the war. I'm sure it's worth something, but Mr Willis assures me it is rubbish. He said, he wouldn't even give me five pounds for it."

Frank picked up the painting, unfortunately he held it upside down in his ignorance. He pretended to admire it. The yellow pear shaped objects in the middle of the canvas, reminded him of a pair of petrol tanks, like the one on his Harley-Davidson. Each was bright buttercup, with a raised petrol cap in its centre.

"Just like a pair of motorbike tanks. Mind you this pair are larger than usual; must be a four gallon model."

She gently removed the frame from his huge hands and turned the picture up, the correct way.

He blushed crimson when he realised the motorbike tanks were actually a large pair of nude female breasts. "Oh yes! That makes all the difference. I'd give you £50 for this picture, any day of the week."

She smiled at him in astonishment, then her cheerful expression slipped to a frown as she noticed the beer-stained string vest and the oily jeans. He didn't look worth fifty pence, let alone fifty pounds!

"Here. I'll take it." Frank pushed the rolled up fifty-pound note into her hand and smiled reassuringly. She hesitated, looked at the money in disbelief and back at her scruffy benefactor.

"Go on, love. It's genuine, honest. I ain't pinched it or anything."

She blushed at his accurate reading of her thoughts, leaned over and gave the big man a kiss on his stubbly cheek and pushed the painting into his hands. Frank was caught off guard by this show of gratitude and blushed deeper than the old lady.

"God bless you, son. That will just pay for my overdue gas bill."

Without another word, she rose from the bench seat and trotted down the High street, her head held high, the spring returned to her step. As she crossed the street, Frank could see she was blowing her nose on her handkerchief and removing an imaginary speck of dust from her eye. He rewrapped the picture in the brown paper and was so pleased with himself, he promptly forgot the dislocation in time and strode into Theo's shop, carrying his prize under one arm.

"Is that the oil painting that old lady just tried to sell to me?" Theo asked sharply, as Frank crossed the doormat. "I just told her it was rubbish. Nothing has changed in the last ten minutes; it still is rubbish. What are you bringing it back in here for?"

Frank realised his mistake and stuttered feebly. "I've...I...I've just bought it...for fifty pounds."

"Then, more fool you!" The antique dealer grunted. "If I were you, I'd stick to clocks. You must know more about them."

Frank halted in the doorway, lost for words and very embarrassed. He turned to leave, thoroughly confused by it all, but unable to believe Theo's attitude. He gave the antique dealer one last broad wink as he left the shop.

"Got something in your eye, Frank?" Theo's voice rang after him along the pavement.

Frank made for the RUFS library, let himself in and climbed the stairs to the attic. He sat down heavily on the clock frame and let out a deep sigh of satisfaction. That was a job well done. The Mr Willis, who was waiting in the future, would be pleased with him. He propped the oil painting beside him on the leather seat and thought over the morning's events. He had enjoyed making that old lady happy. What was it he had said to her?

"It's surprising how things can turn out alright, if you only believe they will...Fancy me giving anyone free advice." Frank was very proud of his bit of homespun philosophy.

Frank rarely thought about anything, other than motorbikes, food, clocks, or his beloved Freda. He sighed again at the reminder of his missing wife.

"It's a pity I can't win the lottery and take her away from all this." A smile crept across his bristly face; a rare inspiration had struck him. Grabbing the newspaper from his back pocket he turned feverishly to the middle pages. There, as usual, was the announcement of the winning lottery numbers. NEXT SATURDAY'S winning lottery numbers!

"Bugger me! That's it! That definitely is it!" The big man rocked back and forth on his seat, unable to contain his excitement. Here was the opportunity to put his marriage problems behind him, once and for all. A large lottery win would give Freda everything she had ever wanted. It might even buy off Gabby; he could offer to pay for the publication of her damn book! Once more, he took the Tempus lever in his big fist and concentrated on Theo's wristwatch.

Ten minutes later in real time, but several days earlier in the cosmic space-time continuum, the clock restorer sauntered nonchalantly into the Runford newsagents. He whistled tunelessly to himself, a nervous habit he developed whenever he was under stress. He sidled up to the lottery counter.

"Am I in time to put a winning ticket into the lottery draw?"

"You should be so lucky!" The assistant laughed aloud at his request.

"Oh...Sorry!" Frank stuttered. "I'm awfully sorry. I was only joking, of course." He huddled in a corner, took the newspaper furtively from his pocket, and copied the winning numbers onto his lottery card. He had just completed his entry when the old lady, who had sold him the oil painting, joined him at the desk.

She adjusted her glasses and smiled with relief, when she focused on the harmless Hell's Angel. As soon as she recognised him, she whispered up to him.

"I'm going to gamble one pound of my pension on the lottery. You never know; you bought my painting for fifty pounds, and one bit of luck might well lead to another."

Frank pushed his card under her nose. "Copy these numbers. I'm feeling 'specially lucky today."

Minutes later, Frank took his ticket to the counter. He fished a pound coin from the depths of his jeans' pocket, blew off the fluff and paid the girl.

"That's the jackpot winner, then," she joked.

Frank stuffed the ticket safely into his pocket and left the shop in a hurry. He was so nervous, he completely forgot to pick up his newspaper, leaving it behind him on the counter top.

After she'd served the old lady, the assistant spotted Frank's paper. She ran out into the street but the restorer had legged it back to the library in a tearing hurry, feeling somehow he had committed a crime and anxious to put distance between himself and the scene of the offence.

The girl walked back into the shop, glanced at the front of the newspaper and frowned. She went straight to the manager's office and spread next week's news in front of him, on the desk.

"Got to be a joke, hasn't it? Is it some kind of spoof newspaper? Must be a made up publicity stunt from one of the publishers."

"Yes, must be."

"But it looks so genuine. Let's see what they report for the lottery numbers." They thumbed through the pages and found the report on the usual page. "I'm half a mind to try these numbers for myself. It's as good a way as any, of picking the winning line. What about it, shall we let all the others in on it? We can use these numbers for our syndicate and have a good laugh when we lose our money as usual."

62

Chapter Twelve

Frank Hogg sat in the deserted attic at the controls of the turret clock, recovering from his journey back in time. He checked Theo's wristwatch and realised he had returned two hours before he had set off. Of course, that's why it seemed so peaceful, Theo was nowhere to be seen; he hadn't arrived at the RUFS library yet. With time to spare, Frank's thoughts turned to another, more pressing problem; his motorbike was damaged and off the road. He needed his transport more than ever, now that Freda had left home. He glanced at the watch again and made a snap decision. Easing the brass Tempus lever forward, he leapt back through time to the day that the farm tractor had knocked him off his trusty Harley-Davidson.

Minutes later, Frank was thumbing a lift home. I could become used to this 'ere time travelling, he thought smugly. I could become sort of addicted. Frank's plan was simple. He would ride his bike into town, exactly as he had on the day of the accident, but this time he would watch out for the tractor and avoid it. He remembered the scene of his accident. It was etched on his memory, right down to the bit where everything went into slow motion and the damn farm machine hit him!

On this rerun of the fateful day, with hindsight, the Hell's Angel braked as he approached the corner and was stationary when the tractor backed out into the road. It missed him by yards.

The driver glanced back as he cleared the gateway and gave Frank a grateful wave, realising they had avoided a collision. Frank drove on into town, humming happily to himself at the success of his plan. At the RUFS library, he ran up the iron staircase and climbed back onto the time machine; he had one more thing to put right:

Big Frank blamed all his recent problems on Gabriella, with some justification. She had stopped speaking to him since the day he refused to make love to her. She had obviously told Freda some lie or other to entice the girl away from him. When Oswald Gotobed had advised him, the Druggist had mentioned Gabriella's corns, but he felt there had to be more to it than just the hard skin on her bony feet. With a rare flash of insight, he wondered if he had upset Gabby by refusing her unwanted offer of sex. Perhaps that was the reason he was in this fix?

Once again Frank travelled back in time, this time to the day Freda attended her meditation class and Gabriella had propositioned him. He made his way home and waited for her to approach him.

Gabby came into his workshop, exactly as she had before. This time he took careful note of everything, He noted the gleam in her eyes and the hungry look on her face. She whipped her dress off, pulling the flimsy Indian cotton over her head. Frank couldn't help noticing her complete lack of underwear. He winced. There was nothing hidden and everything was on display, but it all badly needed ironing! Gabriella threw herself over his workbench, exactly as she had on the previous occasion, but this time his tools and clock parts were not scattered all over the workshop floor; Frank had thoughtfully remembered to clear a space for her before she arrived.

"Make love to me, Frank. You're a big lad and I'm an experienced woman. I'll enjoy your caresses."

Frank looked down at her scrawny backside and his thoughts turned again to scraggy chickens.

The clock restorer couldn't help but notice the odd tufts of hairs springing from the moles on her bottom. She reminded him of a tough old boiling fowl with the feathers inexpertly singed off. She was a very unattractive woman; this was just not going to work out.

Frank was a red-blooded man. He didn't usually need sexual fantasies to get him going, but he was faced with an impossible situation that called for desperate measures.

The single memory most guaranteed to turn Frank on, was the occasion he lost his virginity. It was on his honeymoon. Freda and he had ridden the Harley-Davidson to a motorbike rally in North Wales. They showered in cold water and snuggled together in one large sleeping bag. The earth really moved for him that time; a full ten on the Richter Scale. Their tent collapsed. Their billycan crashed to the floor and the saucepans clanged like all the Welsh church bells, pealing together. The next morning he went straight to the local tattoo parlour and had the name of the nearest town permanently etched on his body. He never wanted to forget where he had experienced such intense feelings of love nor the sight of Freda, her long wet hair sticking to her bare skin.

Keeping this erotic picture of Freda uppermost in his mind, Frank steeled himself for what had to be done. I have travelled back in time just to sort this out, he reminded himself.

Gritting his teeth, the big man grasped Gabriella by her scrawny love handles, pictured Freda's lovely features and thought of England. It took him a long time to sort out the problem to Gabby's satisfaction, but he counted to several thousand and hung on for dear life.

Once her passion was satisfied, Gabriella went up to her room, a stupid smile on her face and an evil glint in her eyes.

Big Frank dragged himself wearily out into the fresh air and made his way back to Runford and the turret clock.

Theo Willis jumped towards the clock frame as it came back into focus, with a sound reminiscent of air escaping from a punctured balloon. He snatched the oil painting from its resting-place on the clock seat and kissed it emotionally. Frank slid himself wearily off the clock frame. He no longer had the energy to get his leg over.

"You were only away ten minutes! How did you manage it so quickly?" Theo enthused, not realising the time machine could deliver Frank back to the attic whenever the restorer chose.

"Only five minutes? I thought that last ride had taken hours!" Frank said without thinking. "Oh! I had ample time to sort out everything, Mr Willis. Now I must get back to me motorbike." His voice was weak but full of hidden meanings.

"Yes, OK, Frank." Theo took the oil painting over to the window to get a better look at it. He glanced out of the library window as he spoke. "Don't worry yourself, Frank. Nobody's taken your bike. I can see it standing safely by the kerb, below us."

Frank bounded over to the window and looked down onto the High Street. His beloved Harley-Davidson stood alongside the pavement, with no sign of any accidental damage. The petrol tank gleamed yellow and pristine in the sunlight as if nothing had ever happened to it.

"Sorry, Mr Willis, must rush." The Hell's Angel ran down the stairs and out into the street to caress his gleaming machine. "You little beauty, you!" He stroked the petrol tank where the dent had been, running his fingers over the perfect steel and the smooth, undamaged contours of the paintwork.

Frank hummed contentedly to himself as he accelerated homewards. He was convinced he would find Freda waiting for him and everything back to normal. He hadn't scorned Gabby the second time around and she certainly seemed grateful for his attentions.

66

Smiling contentedly to himself he leaned into a sharp bend in the road, almost scraping the bike's footrest on the tarmac. Unfortunately his mind was not on the job.

Tantalising glimpses of Freda, naked on their honeymoon, her nipples erect from the cold water, kept dancing before his eyes. With his head full of his wife's charms he lost his concentration and took the corner much too fast.

A farm tractor, backing out of a nearby field, had no chance of avoiding the motorcyclist. There was an instant replay of the previous accident. Frank was not seriously injured but the motorbike tank and forks were badly damaged, exactly as before.

The Hell's Angel lay on his back in the grass field, where the impact had thrown him. He stared grimly up at the blue sky. Surely this had to be fate, or God paying him back for daring to interfere with the normal order of things? On impulse, he thrust his hand into his pocket and took out the leaving note that Freda had left him. The main part of it still read exactly as before but at the bottom was a new postscript.

'PS. I know you humped Gabby. She showed me the bruises and she proved it by describing your tackle. She saw that tattoo you got on your willy, on our honeymoon. She knows it reads Llandudno and not just Ludo.'

"Shit!" Frank collapsed in despair, rolling the back of his crash helmet and his ponytail in a ripe cowpat.

Chapter Thirteen.

"I'm going down to my cellar workshop. I see no sense in wasting time up here in the dispensary, now the morning rush is over." Oswald Gotobed made his excuses and left his brother to dispense the last of the prescriptions.

Down in the laboratory, where Oswald studied his magic, coffee was already brewing over a Bunsen burner. Oswald took his weather magic files from the bookshelf. He had made a study of climatic spells for some years, becoming proficient enough to ensure fine weather when some local outdoor event needed it, and helping his own business by prolonging the fine summer weather. This allowed the South Lincolnshire farmers to gather the harvest, a service gratefully rewarded by free sacks of potatoes and braces of pheasants, whenever he asked for them. It also meant the pharmacy sold out of suntan preparations during the late spell of holiday sunshine, releasing their working capital.

Oswald thumbed through his well-worn copy of a correspondence course on weather control; an American publication he had bought second-hand from the Exchange and Mart, and muttered to himself as he searched.

"Let me see...fine weather...here we are, next to the Red Indian rain dances." He poured a black coffee, helped himself to a lettuce sandwich and settled down to study the text, but he was soon interrupted.

Roger called down the stairs. "Mr Oswald, police sergeant Peele is in the shop. He's asking to see you."

Oswald smiled slyly to himself; he had been expecting this visit. He might have kidded other people that it was his extra sensory perception that had forewarned him, but as Peele was secretary to the Allotment Holders association and they were holding their annual show very soon.. It was a visit he had been expecting. The sergeant would be after a guarantee of fine weather for the day of the show.

"Do come down, Peele." The High Wizard beckoned the policeman to join him in the cellar. "What can I do for you? I don't suppose you are here in your capacity as RUFS secretary." Peel was also secretary to the Runford Union of Fenland Slodgers; he collected these offices like some folk collect pot Toby Jugs. The policeman felt it helped him keep his finger on the pulse of the town.

"Correct. It's about the horticultural show."

Oswald smirked to himself; he had been right in his assumption.

"I expect you want me to conjure up fine weather yet again? It docs ensure your gate takings are up."

"The committee have instructed me to approach you, as we did last year. But, left to me, I wouldn't waste my time." Peele grunted. "I don't believe in this nonsense. I'm sure we'd have fine weather without all this mumbo-jumbo from the High Wizard of the RUFS." His personal feelings voiced, the policeman folded his arms firmly across his barrel chest and stuck out his chin aggressively.

Oswald shook his head sadly. He should have anticipated trouble from the straight-laced policeman.

"Can't we negotiate a price? After all, the show brings in most of the club's annual revenue, and a downpour could ruin the day."

"How much?" Peele asked sharply.

"Well, as a special concession, I would settle for a complimentary ticket to the show and all the free beer I can drink in the member's bar tent."

"That will cost a packet! The amount of ale you pour down your throat when you are paying for it is considerable; I can imagine what you'd do if it was free. No. I've made up my mind. I'm not paying you one penny, in cash or kind. You would be getting our money under false pretences."

The sergeant looked Oswald straight in the eyes and wagged an accusing finger at him. "It might even be against the law. Any more of this and I'll charge you with something criminal."

"Come on now, be realistic, man! How can you think of taking me to court? Can you see yourself explaining to the presiding magistrate how I make magic spells to affect the weather? You'd be laughed out of the courtroom. The local paper would make a meal of it. Imagine what your chief constable would say when he read the reports."

Peele scowled at the Druggist, turned on his heels and stomped up the stairs to the sales floor. "I'm not paying you one penny. I'll not waste any more of my valuable time with you."

"I only hope you've brought your umbrella with you." Oswald shouted after the retreating officer.

As soon as the policeman had left the laboratory, Oswald got to work.

"I'll teach that arrogant twit a lesson he'll never forget." The Wizard muttered as he opened the page on Apache Rain Dances. These were reputed to be the best spells for wet weather production, in a hurry.

70

He sang the words tunelessly, waved a dinner knife above his head as a makeshift tomahawk, and stuck a Cos lettuce leaf behind each ear in imitation of an Eagle-feather head dress.

Up in the High Street, it was a fine day. The sun shone down on Runford. There wasn't a cloud in the sky. Sergeant Peele lingered in the pharmacy to do some shopping for his wife and to buy some indigestion tablets for himself. He thanked Malcolm for his help and methodically placed his change into his deep leather purse. He hesitated as he reached the door, stuffed his bag of goods into his pocket, and was about to step into the street, when there was a loud clap of thunder. Above him, black storm clouds billowed and mushroomed like smoke from burning car tyres. It reminded him of a speeded up film of the onset of the Indian monsoons. He frowned and tutted to himself. Suddenly the entire street lit up with a blinding lightning flash. He stepped back into the chemist shop and stared glumly out at the darkened street.

It rained bucketfuls. Steely rods of water rattled on the tarmac surface of the market place. It bounced off the pavement, soaking everyone caught out in it. Gutters ran like rivers. The drains could not cope with the volume of the downpour. Shallow lakes formed in the middle of the road. A flash of lightning struck a waste bin, sending a shower of empty beer cans, chip papers and banana skins up into the damp air. Peele cowered back into the pharmacy and waited for it to stop.

Oswald sauntered up the cellar stairs and stood behind the chemist counter with a grin on his face as he watched the unusual weather.

"You needn't smirk! This is a perfectly natural occurrence, and nothing whatsoever to do with you." Peele growled, but there was a touch of doubt in his voice.

"I think you should have brought your sledge with you. I do hope the horticultural show doesn't have this kind of weather."

The Wizard turned on his heels and returned to his workshop.

The rain abated. Police sergeant Peele stood in the doorway, anxious to be on his way, but he couldn't help mulling over Oswald's last comments as he waited.

Down below the shop, Oswald concentrated feverishly on cold weather production. He recited the appropriate Latin spell at breakneck speed and focussed all his psychic energy.

In the marketplace, the air went suddenly chilly. The temperature dropped rapidly and the raindrops slowed down in their descent. They began to drift in the wind as they turned to large white snowflakes. Suddenly the wind howled and a blizzard blew up. The customers in the pharmacy found it impossible to see to the other side of the square through a thick blanket of hailstones as big as golf balls. The hail rattled on the shop windows and beat against the broken waste bin.

"Lets shut the door and keep that lot outside." Malcolm hastily pushed the front door shut. Peele scowled, hunched his shoulders, and thrust his hands deep into his pockets. Slowly, he turned away from the window and made for the cellar steps. Even he could no longer deny the evidence of his own eyes.

"Come in, Peele." Oswald's voice rang out before the policeman reached the laboratory door. "What is it this time? Can I do anything for you?"

"Perhaps I was a bit hasty. I've had time to think. Perhaps the committee was right to ask you to ensure fine weather for the show...not that I personally think you can do anything about it, you understand. But if they want to be that gullible, I ought to bow to their wishes."

"Good! I thought you might. I'm not a vindictive person. I'll do my best, as I have in other years. I only ask for a free ticket and my fill of beer in return."

Peele reluctantly agreed. They shook hands on the deal and he promised to hand over the free pass on the day of the show, fine weather permitting.

Outside in the High Street, things returned to normal. The sun came out again and the black clouds miraculously dissolved. The pavements steamed and the puddles began to evaporate in the warmth. Very soon it looked as if nothing unusual had happened, the only evidence of the freak weather being the upturned litter bin. Oswald escorted the Allotment Holder's secretary from the shop, rubbing his hands together and smiling as if he had just won a free holiday. The Wizard had already been approached by the Horticultural Society to make fine weather for their show on the coming weekend. Now he had the contract for both events.

Chapter Fourteen.

The very same morning that Frank Hogg launched his career in time travelling, John Buttadaeus left his lodgings early. He walked through the bar as the landlady was tidying the bar top.

"Mrs Postlethwaite, help I need. A Mr Gotobed, do you know him?" John had remembered the unusual name of Gotobed, from the news item Omni had recited to him. This was an important lead and one he intended to follow. It was a Mr Gotobed who had briefed the newspapers after the vegetable show; the man who announced the winning tomatoes was an everlasting variety, developed by genetic engineering. This man must know something about the subject.

"Do you mean Malcolm Gotobed the Chemist, or his brother Oswald the Druggist?" Lydia put down her duster in mid polish and smiled sweetly at her lodger, praying he would understand her explanation.

"Are there two of them? The one I seek is interested in plants and vegetables. Him I mean."

"Then it's Malcolm you're after. He's the one everybody consults when they've blackspot on their roses or whitefly on their lettuces. Malcolm's the gardening expert; Oswald is useless on gardening, he's more your contraceptive expert, or home brewing guru."

Lydia's lodger hesitated. He recalled he had met a Mr Gotobed in the churchyard when he first arrived in Runford. That particular gentleman was a small person in khaki shorts and a wide brimmed hat. He was unforgettable.

"This Malcolm person, a scout master, would he be? A small round man in short trousers and a sun hat? I met him at the churchyard. It was he who your hostelry recommended to me."

"Ah! I'd heard the rumours that Malcolm was abroad that evening in some sort of fancy dress? I wondered if he had stolen those clothes from my neighbours washing line. I mentioned it to the police when they came to make enquiries about the missing boiler suit and pink, angora cardigan. But, from all accounts, he was done up like an antique, boy-scout!"

John frowned at this information, and was about to leave by the main door, when Lydia stopped him and handed him a folded piece of paper.

"Sorry to remind you about my bill, dear, but I could do with the money."

The lodger plunged his hand into his jacket pocket and took out a handful of small change. Lydia stared open mouthed at the collection of five pence pieces, buttons and foreign coins.

"Looks like the collection plate at the church." She joked, to hide her embarrassment.

"No. Not the collection plate. It was the Poor Box." John solemnly corrected her.

Lydia broke into a hearty laugh and slapped her sides appreciatively.

"That wasn't at all a bad attempt at a joke, for someone with your limited English." She looked into his face but her twinkling eyes met a stony, serious stare. "Perhaps it wasn't so damn funny after all." She conceded, under her breath.

"These monies you require. Show me."

"Lydia opened the till and took out £70 in used ten-pound notes.

She held up a single note for him to see. Poor dear, she thought, he hasn't learned how to use our currency yet. I will not confuse him with fives and twenties.

"I borrow this." John took one of the ten pound notes and went back up stairs. In his room, John locked the door securely and switched Omni on.

"Make me fifty of these." He commanded. The black box hummed happily as it extracted the necessary molecules to copy paper and ink, from its surroundings. It did not stop until it had manufactured fifty perfect copies of the ten-pound note, correct in every detail, right down to the coffee stain. The old man took two garments from his wardrobe and concealed them in a carrier bag, then he hurried down to the bar, plastic bag in one hand and money in the other.

"Here. You take what you need." He handed over the complete roll of notes.

Lydia took her original note, counted seventy pounds from the bundle and gave the remainder back to her lodger.

He smiled gratefully, then insisted. "I still require to find this Chemist. I must speak words with him. Where is he?"

"Malcolm will be at the Chemist shop on the High Street...If it's just a headache you've developed, I can help, dear. If it's a couple of Aspirin tablets you need, I always keep a bottle in my medicine cabinet, in case one of my regulars gets a hangover. A single dose of two tablets usually does the trick."

"Dear lady, thank you, no." He clicked his heels, gave a slight nod of his grey head and left the pub.

Roger the chemists' trainee was on duty at the till when the elderly stranger marched into the pharmacy. He stood to attention as John Buttadaeus came to a halt at the counter.

"A bottle of Aspirins, I need. The small chemist, Mr Gotobed, is he in?" He asked for the pain killers only as an excuse to speak to the chemist, much as a nervous lad might ask to see the toothpaste when he really needed advice on condoms.

76

Roger was an intelligent lad and realised a stranger may not know there were two Mr Gotobeds, both pharmacists and identical to look at. He tried to think of a tactful way to find out which of his employers the man wanted to see.

"Did you want to see the Chemist or the Druggist?" He asked hopefully.

"The small, round man with the short, brown trousers and the wide hat, I require. He a scout master appears to be."

Roger had heard the rumours about his employer's appearance at the scout meeting. He stifled a snigger and shouted for Mr Malcolm.

"There's a gentleman asking for you , Mr Malcolm."

"Ah, my friend. Are you settled at the Dog in a Doublet?" Malcolm smiled affably over the counter and held out his hand in greeting.

"Thank you, yes. Some more advice I require." He ignored the outstretched hand of friendship and seemed to be searching his memory for the right words.

"He needs a bottle of Aspirins," Roger piped up helpfully.

"How many? We stock them in bottles of 50 or 100."

"That seems for too many. Two, I think."

"Two hundred?"

"One bottle of two tablets, if you please. Just two tablets. The usual dose is that not?"

Malcolm glanced quickly at the trainee, who was standing open mouthed at the till. It was the first time Roger had heard anyone ask for a bottle of just two Aspirin tablets. The Chemist did not want to upset his customer so he smiled knowingly and nodded his agreement. It wouldn't do for customers to think the staff were laughing at them. It would be bad for business. He coloured up red at the thought and wrung his hands.

"Quite right, Sir. It's no use buying too many drugs." Malcolm hurriedly tried to cover up his embarrassment. "I agree with you, Sir. Buy exactly the amount you need. If you tell me your name I will dispense two tablets for you from my dispensary stock, put them in a click-locked container and label them accordingly."

"John Buttadaeus." The man clicked his heels, inclined his head again and introduced himself, enunciating the words slowly and methodically. Malcolm confirmed the spelling of this foreign sounding name and retreated into the dispensary to pack the two aspirins.

Roger, intrigued by this unusual customer, put his head around the dispensary screen and mouthed. "What are you going to charge him? Two tablets can't be worth very much, can they?"

Malcolm handed over the bottle of two tablets to his customer and apologised. "The bottle costs more than the contents. I'm afraid I'll have to charge you ten pence to cover it."

John Buttadaeus pulled a handful of ten-pound notes from his pocket and piled them on the counter. The Chemist stared at this offering in amazement, until it dawned on him the customer must have no experience of English currency.

"I'll take it out of one of these." He helped himself to a single coffee stained note.

"Take all you need. Plenty more I can manufacture."

Malcolm laughed aloud and looked up from the till to show he appreciated the joke. It was a brave attempt at humour for so obvious a foreigner. His gaze met a blank expression.

"Well, perhaps it wasn't so funny, after all." He mumbled lamely, shrugging his shoulders and grinning sheepishly at Roger. Just to be safe he held the ten-pound note up to the light to check its authenticity.

"Some information, I need." John came to the real reason for his visit.

Malcolm handed over the change and assumed his attentive look; the face he always saved for consultations.

"This vegetable show you advertise, who will win the cup for best tomatoes?"

Malcolm raised his eyebrows imperceptibly, nothing too obvious for he was beginning to expect these unusual questions from this stranger. "That depends. The judges will decide on the day. But, Greenfingers Clay, the head gardener at the Hall, has won that class for the past ten years. I suppose he has to be favourite."

"Greenfingers Clay, say you?"

"That's the man; a very competent gardener. Very jealous of his reputation, he is. He'll want to retain his unbeaten record. If I were a betting man, which God forbid, I'm not, I'd put my money on him."

"The Hall? Where is this hall?"

"It's a big Victorian mansion. The first house you pass on your right, if you leave the town on the Fen Road. It's set back from the road with a wide gravelled drive. You can't miss it."

Malcolm was about to ask why the old gentleman wanted to know all these things, for the Hall was never open to the public, being the country home of the local Member of Parliament; an ambitious man with some obscure job in the Ministry of Defence. They certainly did not welcome casual visitors. The grounds of the house were patrolled by security guards with fierce dogs. Malcolm was about to suggest it was not a good idea to visit the Hall, when a high pitched, electronic bleeping filled the shop. The Chemist and his trainee looked at each other in surprise.

John Buttadaeus reached into his inside pocket and took out a small black matchbox, which was still bleeping madly and flashing a red light.

"Silence, Omni!" The shrill noise ceased abruptly, leaving a wonderful silence in its wake.

"Portable telephone or personal pager, is it?" Malcolm asked, curiously.

"Your own business, mind!" The old man grunted, then marched out of the pharmacy without another word.

"What a rude old man." Roger blurted out, as soon as the door close and he knew the customer was out of earshot. Malcolm went very red and tutted silently to himself. He was of the opinion that bad manners were unforgivable, but he was too well mannered to say so, out loud. He went back into the dispensary and glanced at the printer screen, which had the aspirin label still showing on it.

"John Buttadaeus? I've met that name before." He murmured curiously. "Funny how some names can stick in your memory. I know I've read it recently, somewhere." He tried to recall exactly where he had seen the foreign sounding name. Was it in the Book of Saint, he'd borrowed from the vicar? Was it in the Parish Magazine? Malcolm closed his eyes and tried to recall all the books he had borrowed from the library that month.

"That's it, Roger!" He shouted jubilantly. He prided himself on his keen memory.

"Whatever's the matter, Mr Gotobed?"

"John Buttadaeus. That's the name given to a mysterious, historical character who turned up in Antwerp in the thirteenth century. He was seen again in the fifteenth century and in the sixteenth. On that last occasion he had with him a portrait of himself painted by Titian, who had been dead for 130 years!"

"The same man?"

"Yes, so it seems. I've been reading the Legend of the Wandering Jew. He is supposed to have insulted Jesus on his way to Calvary. Our Lord cursed him to wander the earth until the second coming."

"You think that man is the Wandering Jew? He looks old, but not that old, surely?"

80

"Don't be silly, Roger. I only said he has the same name. We both know it would be impossible for the same man to keep popping up throughout history. That would be a miracle, or some kind of time travel." They laughed together at such a ridiculous idea.

Once he had left the chemists shop, John Buttadaeus dodged down a deserted alleyway and took Omni from his pocket.

"Well? Why the panic, Omni? "

"The time machine has been used, master. And it has been activated twice more since I bleeped you."

"Is it safely back now?"

"Yes, master."

"Some fool must have caught the levers! Someone like that fat idiot who wore the twentieth century onion sack as a vest. This is happening too often. I must immobilise the machine before we lose it. Lead me to its hiding place."

Frank Hogg and Theo Willis were just leaving the RUFS library when the grey haired stranger crossed the High Street. Neither of them noticed the old man, for they were too engrossed in their own affairs; Theo was admiring his valuable oil painting; Frank only had eyes for his reborn Harley-Davidson.

The time traveller waited until the street was empty, then used Omni to check the Union premises for other life forms. It took only minutes to enter the building, make his way up to the attic, and find the hidden time machine. Five more minutes work and he was leaving the building with the two brass levers safely concealed in his jacket pocket. Without the controls the turret clock would be going nowhere. He could now concentrate on his quest for the everlasting tomatoes, with no worries about his transport home.

As it was a pleasant afternoon, John decided to take a stroll along the Fen Road. He walked by the Dog in a Doublet and out of town, looking for the Hall, where Greenfingers Clay was head gardener.

81

He noted with satisfaction, as he passed by the pub, that Lydia's neighbour was standing in his garden, hands on hips, staring open mouthed at his dungarees and his wife's pink cardigan, mysteriously returned to his washing line. John patted the empty carrier bag in his pocket. The last thing he wanted was trouble with the local police.

Chapter Fifteen.

The Hall was a rambling redbrick house, with a high wall fronting the Fen Road and heavy cast iron gates sealing the driveway off from the outside world. John arrived just as the council dustcart was leaving. He waited and watched as a burly security guard directed the dustcart onto the road. Once the vehicle was clear of the driveway, the gates were closed and firmly locked.

John held up his hand to the driver of the refuse lorry and shouted to him. "The Hall, is that it?"

"Sure is, mate."

"Tell me. How does one get in?"

"One doesn't, mate! Unless one is invited, or one is doing some work for 'em."

John frowned, shaking his head in disappointment.

"Who ya looking for, mate?"

"Mr Clay, the gardener."

"Ah! Old Greenfingers; 'e hangs out in the 'all gardens. Go down the side road to the back of the 'ouse. There's a gate in the wall about half way down. Ya can't miss it." The driver revved up his engine and drove off towards town, with a cloud of black exhaust and bluebottle flies following in his wake.

John strolled past the front of the house, keeping a weather eye on the security guard and his large Alsation dog, who were stationed in the grounds where they could keep watch on the main road through the bars of the gate.

He took the first side turning and strolled alongside the high wall for a further half a mile until he reached the gate to an enclosed garden. There was no one in sight in the garden, but just to be sure, he switched on Omni to check the coast was clear. The box bleeped a warning.

"Four legged life form approaching the gate, master."

John leaned forward to look closer into the estate. Sure enough, there was another German Shepherd dog lurking on the pathway, its ears pricked up and its teeth bared, alert to a stranger's presence.

"Call him over to the gate, Omni."

The box emitted a high pitched whistle, too faint for any human ears to detect, but the dog heard it and came to investigate. As soon as the animal reached the gate, Omni changed the note to an even higher pitch. The dog whined and lay on the path, both paws covering its ears. John leaned over the gate and briefly touched the Alsation under its collar. The animal fell instantly into a deep sleep.

"That's taken care of him. Anymore life forms nearby?"

"Nothing, master."

John crept stealthily into the Hall gardens, hesitating at every step, looking to left and right, intent on finding the everlasting tomato plants before he was detected. He walked for what seemed miles, for the old garden was immense; being set out in Victorian times when the owners employed scores of gardeners and entertained on a lavish scale. Now there was only Greenfingers Clay and a lad on a government, training scheme. John tiptoed around the corner of a large greenhouse and came face to face with this spotty youth. The lad had a muck fork in his hand and suspicion written all over his acned face.

"Who are you, mate? What are y'after?"

"The Ministry of Vegetables I work for. The prize tomatoes I am here to inspect." John thought he would try bluffing his way to his quarry, as the lad looked non-too bright.

"Oh arr! Who said you could wander 'round Mr Clay's garden? 'e ain't said nothing to me about the Minister coming. Anyway, ya don't look like the regular vicar."

"Maybe he forgot." John sidled up to the boy, put up his hand as if to brush off some dirt from the lad's shoulder, and gently touched his neck, immobilising him, just as he had the guard dog.

"Now for the prize tomatoes. You will lead me to them; the one's that will win at the vegetable show."

The trainee gardener turned slowly like a sleepwalker, pushed his fork prongs into the heap of manure, and led his attacker back towards the gate, where the largest greenhouse stood. Throwing open the doors he gestured inside.

John stepped through the entrance, anticipation written all over his face. The warm, moist smell of growing tomato plants tickled his nostrils. He stopped just inside the doorway, his eyes wide and his mouth agape with surprise. The glasshouse was immense and it contained row upon row of tomato vines, all heavy with fruit. There must have been millions of them!

"Which ones?" He asked curtly.

"The best ones on the day of the show." The lad explained in a dreamy, far-off voice.

John Buttadaeus cursed in his native tongue and mumbled to Omni. "This is going to be more difficult than I ever anticipated. I can't possibly steal a million tomatoes! How do I get my hands on the winning fruit?" Omni sighed but made no useful suggestions. John grew impatient. "I must have just the ones that are everlasting. Can they all be genetically altered fruit? Scan them for me, Omni."

The little box buzzed busily like a demented bee trapped in a crisp packet, then reported its findings.

85

"All fruit are identical, master. I have no way of predicting if they will rot with time. Common sense suggests you pick some and store them a day or two to see."

John glared darkly at his robot; computerised sarcasm was not welcome. Omni kept very quiet. Ignoring the robot's suggestion, John thought the problem through. Which tomatoes should he pick? There were so many possibilities. He couldn't decide. In frustration he gave up and stormed out of the greenhouse, leaving the mesmerised lad wandering among the plants like a lost explorer in a humid rain forest. John slammed the door behind him and made for the gate.

"I'll wait until the day of the show. The basket of fruit that Mr Clay enters for the competition, will be the one to analyse." He whispered to Omni.

He left the garden the way he had entered it, knowing the trances he had inflicted on the dog and the boy, would wear off with no ill effects, but leaving them with no memory of their visitors.

Chapter Sixteen.

Theo Willis was overjoyed. All was well in the dealer's avaricious world. He had bought a valuable Picasso for a mere fifty pounds and had immediately telephoned a top London museum to arrange to sell it to them for a fortune.

His wife noticed his unusually good humour, for he was normally a grumpy individual, only smiling when he'd managed to twist some unsuspecting client out of his money. She hadn't a clue why he was so cheerful, but she decided to cash in on the mood while it lasted.

"Theo, dear. You know I need a new hat for my niece's wedding..." She got no further.

"Have two, dear. Get yourself some shoes, handbag and a suit to match. You deserve it." He smiled happily at her. If such cheap trifles pleased her, he could well afford to keep her sweet; he was getting a fortune for that oil painting. Anyway, he needed to be in her good books so there would be no objections when he spent the bulk of the money on himself.

Simon Smith, the Picasso expert from the National Museum of Modern Painters' in London, called that same afternoon. He agreed, it did appear to be an unlisted masterpiece from the master's Yellow Period. He took the painting away with him to check with the restoration experts at the museum.

At Theo's request, he supplied a written receipt for the canvas.

"I'm sure the investigations are just a formality, old boy; just routine pigment analysis and x-ray examination. I'd stake my international reputation on the authenticity of this Picasso. It is, without doubt, genuine. As you say, it's worth at least two million pounds sterling." Simon Smith oozed charm as he wrapped the canvas and took it away.

The antique dealer poured himself another large glass of fifty-year-old Malt, from the bottle he'd been saving for just such an occasion, and sank back into his armchair with a self-satisfied sigh. He looked up at the ceiling and pictured what he would do with all that money.

"Congratulations are in order. Theo, you are a clever old devil. This time you've excelled yourself." He drank a toast to himself and thumbed through a selection of brochures he had picked up in town. He glowered over the Exotic Singles Holiday leaflets from the travel agent, and the Porsche catalogue he had collected from the garage. The time travel ruse had worked like a charm. Frank Hogg was too stupid to realise what he had done, and the old lady was no doubt grateful for her fifty pounds. He had no conscience about the matter. After all, she had originally asked fifty pounds for her painting; so everyone was satisfied. It had all been so easy. There were rich pickings for the asking, in this system of getting rare antiques from the past.

After his third glass of the Malt, Theo began to envisage further trips into the past. Perhaps Frank could visit France and collect a Van Gogh or two? It was common knowledge that nobody wanted the artist's work in his lifetime. Many of his canvases were swapped for a meagre meal and a glass of house wine. Vincent would probably give his right ear for a free ham sandwich and enough centimes to buy a full carafe of plonk.

"Just half a dozen Sunflower studies. No sense in getting too greedy." Theo dreamed.

He would have to invent a good yarn to fool Frank Hogg into working for him again, but Frank was a simple enough fellow; he was easily led.

"Perhaps a Turner or two. A couple of Gainsborough landscapes and a Holbein." The choice was endless. The only limit to his acquisitions was his imagination.

"How will I spend all this new-found wealth? Perhaps I'll get a facelift? Join the 18 to 90 cruises for swinging millionaires? Have a garage bursting at the seams with expensive sports cars? Divorce the wife and change the replacement model every time I change my car?" The sound of the door closing as Mrs Willis returned from her shopping spree, silenced his wishful thinking.

She paraded her new outfit in front of her drunken husband. He nodded happily, waving his hands expansively in the air. If she was happy, his plan had worked. He went to mop his sweating brow, pulled a red silk handkerchief from his top pocket with an exaggerated flourish and catapulted the receipt for the oil painting, across the room.

Mrs Willis, who was stone cold sober, caught the priceless piece of paper in mid air. She unfolded it curiously.

"Receipt for one Picasso oil painting. Signed Albert Steptoe and Son?" She grinned at the joke.

Theo sobered up instantly. That remark was like a bucket of ice-cold water on the back of his neck. He threw down his glass and snatched the receipt from her. Sure enough, when he managed to focus his eyes on it, the signature was not Simon Smith. It appeared to be Albert Steptoe, the fictional rag and bone man off the Television! There was no mistaking it, even though Theo read it a hundred times.

"Must be a coincidence! Must be a similar name...I'll ring the museum."

The London Museum of Modern Painters had never heard of Albert Steptoe. And they had no record of Theo's oil painting. Neither had they sent a representative to Runford to undertake a valuation.

"It's possible our Mr Simon Smith dealt with it. He may have forgotten to pass on the message as he was going on holiday. It appears he was the only one in the office at the time you claim to have telephoned us. I can't help you any further because he's left no details and he's away now."

"Where? When will he be back? How can I contact him?" Theo shouted down the telephone.

"Impossible to say...he left rather suddenly...he rang in and said something about a long overdue sabbatical... I understand he's taken leave of absence to go abroad for a year or two to do some research on Picasso."

The antique dealer poured out another tumbler of whiskey, and rounded on his wife, who was still happily posing in front of a cheval mirror, drifting dreamily along the carpet like an overweight supermodel on the catwalk.

"You can take that bloody lot back to the shops, for a start! Do you think I'm made of money?"

Towards evening, when Theo had drunk himself silly and partially sobered up again, he had a sudden brainwave. He would go back in time to that afternoon and refuse to let Smith take the painting away with him. He would wait until after dark, then let himself into the library and ride the Time Machine himself. The effects of the Malt ensured he had enough Dutch courage to consider such a reckless thing.

The church clock struck ten. Theo sidled out of Church House. Lucky for him, his wife was still locked in her bedroom, sobbing her heart out on the duvet; she would be no wiser. Nonchalantly he drifted across the High Street, keeping to the shadows, avoiding the drunks arguing with the yobs outside the fish shop, and let himself into the Union library.

Theo did not switch on the lights inside the building, not wishing to attract attention. The attic was not wired for electricity and the window was too small to let in much light, so he had to feel his way in the pitch black. He stumbled from the top step of the spiral staircase towards the turret clock.

"Damn!" In the dark, he found the iron frame with his shinbone! He struck a match and peered about him. The leather seat was just to his right. He slid onto it, swearing yet again as the match burned down to his finger's ends. "Calm yourself," he told himself severely. "This is no time to panic. Two million quid is at stake." He struck another match and searched for the brass control levers he had seen Frank Hogg use.

Fifteen minutes later, surrounded by charred matchsticks, his entire box of matches nearly spent, he was in tears. The levers had proved impossible to find. Nothing was going to plan for him. He sat glumly in the black of the attic and tried to gather his thoughts.

Bang! Downstairs a door slammed! Someone else was in the Union building! Theo sat frozen to the turret clock, hardly daring to breathe. Who could it be at this late hour? His eyes grew large and round as he stared into the inky darkness, half expecting someone to appear. Heavy footsteps echoed below him across the library. It occurred to him then, it could be Oswald Gotobed doing some late reading, but there was no sign of a light being switched on. Maybe it was a burglar? The thought of violence struck terror into the cowardly antique dealer.

As Theo sat on the leather seat, paralysed in fear of his life, he heard furtive footsteps creeping up the treads of the iron staircase. Someone was coming up the stairs towards him!

The intruder reached the top step and stepped onto the wooden attic floor. The creak of floorboards and the rasp of laboured breathing were amplified by the darkness.

Theo was petrified as the intruder eased his way across the attic towards him.

Suddenly, a bright light bit through the blackness The torch beam blinded the frightened antique dealer.

"Good God! Mr Willis! What are you doing here?" A man's deep voice shouted in alarm. The torch clattered to the floor and immediately plunged the room back into inky darkness.

Theo fumbled with his last match. With shaking fingers, he struck it against the box and held the flame in front of him. In the wavering yellow light, he found himself face to face with the stubbly jowls of Frank Hogg!

Chapter Seventeen.

Saturday dawned in bright sunshine. Oswald had ensured a fine day for the first of the produce shows by weaving his weather magic, for a fee of one free ticket and all the beer he could drink.

Roger was excited. He awoke at first light, cycled to his boss's garden and picked his precious tomato crop. Twenty ripe fruit were required to compete in the tomato class at the show. He had exactly that number. He polished each one lovingly with a new, yellow duster and placed it on a pad of cotton wool in a wicker basket, handling each one with the care he would have lavished on a fragile, bird's egg.

Oswald, still in his dressing gown, paisley pyjamas and slippers, walked down to the greenhouse to offer his good wishes. He knew the lad stood as much chance as a one legged skier in the Olympics, but the Druggist was in a good mood. He had wangled the day off work, and there was the prospect of as much free ale as he could drink.

"They don't look too bad." Oswald admitted, surprise showing in his voice.

"I'm pleased with them, Mr Gotobed. Especially as it's my first effort."

In the main tent at the park, all was bustle and preparation. The WI was setting up their Tropical Garden in a Matchbox competition; miniature cacti, tiny pot camels and bags of silver sand were everywhere.

The flower, fruit and vegetable growers were arranging their entries with the care of florists at a royal wedding. Clay had entered every category in the vegetable show and his produce was magnificent; especially his tomatoes. In fact, his crop of Moneymaker was so good, no one else felt like competing against him. Fully-grown men wiped tears from their eyes and pushed their own puny tomatoes back into their bicycle saddle bags. They could not stomach the thoughts of inevitable defeat.

Roger, oblivious to all these undercurrents, arranged his precious crop, in a wicker show basket on the judging table.

"I wouldn't bother, lad." A disappointed grower nudged the lad's elbow, shook his head sadly, and nodded knowingly towards Clay's perfect Tomatoes.

Roger grinned. He was proud to be showing at all. To him, it was like taking part in the Olympic Games; competing was enough; winning had not entered his young head.

At nine o'clock sharp, the tent was emptied. All the competitors had to leave so that the judging committee could deliberate in private. Most of the men cleared off to the beer tent. The ladies went to the WI reception for a cheese and wine tasting. The judges walked amongst the deserted tables, discussing each entry, pinning certificates and rosettes on the ones that found their favour. They chatted knowledgeably about Turnips, Potatoes and Cos Lettuces. Roger left with the others but he was too excited to go far. He stood just outside the exit flap so that he could rush back immediately the judging was over.

John Buttadaeus, trying to look inconspicuous, preceded the committee around the tent, looking for the everlasting tomatoes. A steward challenged him, but hearing his thick foreign accent and being convinced the intruder couldn't understand a word he was saying, decided it was easier to leave him in peace.

"Omni. Find the tomatoes. Quickly." John hissed into his black box.

"Near the exit, master."

"John sauntered to the table and was surprised to find only two entries for that category. His task was made easy. One glance convinced him that Clay's fruit was by far the best. He knew from Omni's data banks that the winning tomatoes would be the everlasting variety, so he deftly swept the Hall's entry into his carrier bag and left by the side exit. So quickly was the deed done, no one noticed. The thief almost bumped into Roger in his haste to escape.

The judges were disappointed in the poor entry for the tomato class; only one competitor. They debated whether to award the Silver cup at all, as it was such a poor turn out. The vicar, who was chairman, reminded his committee of their duty.

"The rules state the best entry will be awarded the cup. As we have only one sample of tomatoes, it must be the best. Much as I deplore this lack of interest, we have no choice. Let's have no more arguments." They pinned the prestigious red ribbon and the first-prize certificate onto Roger's basket of fruit and moved on to the next long table.

"Ah! The Tropical Garden in a Matchbox..." His voice trailed off as he realised the number of entries for this WI competition. In contrast to the tomatoes, this section had attracted hundreds of entries; every member of the Runford WI had had a crack at it.

"Perhaps it was a Godsend we spent so little time on the tomatoes." The chairman raised his eyes to the top of the tent and put his hands together in thanks.

Oswald was propping up the bar in the beer tent when his trainee rushed in to find him.

"I've won! I have won! Mr Gotobed." Roger almost knocked the beer glass from his boss's fingers.

"Never! You've never beaten Greenfingers Clay! You've actually won the Silver Cup?"

Roger blushed. "I've beaten no one. Mine was the only entry."

Oswald creased his brow in disbelief and put down his pint tankard. He followed the lad back to the marquee to see for himself.

There on the table he found Roger's basket of fruit, in splendid isolation. The winner's rosette was pinned firmly to it. Over by the entrance, he could hear Greenfingers Clay arguing loudly with the judges.

"I tell you, I left my basket of tomatoes beside that lads. Your stewards were responsible for its safekeeping. What are you going to do about it? Foul play; that's what I call it."

"Look here, Clay. Sorry as I am at this incident, You have won every other first prize in the fruit and vegetable classes. Can't you be satisfied with that? There's always next year."

Greenfingers gave in grumpily. The Silver Cup for the best tomatoes had stood in pride of place on his mantelpiece for years; now his wife would have to shuffle the other trophies about, to hide the gap.

"I'm gonna report this to the police, you know." He walked away in disgust.

Sergeant Peele, who was on the committee, just grinned reassurance at the chairman.

"I'll beat you at the next show." Clay hissed in Roger's ear, as he passed by the lad.

"I won't be entering the next show, will I. There aren't any tomatoes left on my plant."

John Buttadaeus, his mission accomplished, made his way swiftly to his lodgings at the Dog in a Doublet, and locked himself in his room. He placed the tomatoes on his bedside cabinet and grinned with pleasure.

"Well, Omni, I've done it! I have the secret of eternal life firmly in my grasp."

Omni stayed silent.

"Don't you think I'm a genius?" John glared at the silent black box, demanding an answer.

"Of course, master. There is no argument about that."

"What do you think of my tomatoes?"

The miniature computer scanned the fruit thoroughly. "They appear to be just ordinary Moneymaker tomatoes; nothing exceptional about them; just common or garden greenhouse produce."

"Nonsense! They are everlasting. Tonight we can go forward to our own time. I can leave these primitive people and I can complete my work on my immortality."

Omni replied not a word. It just tutted quietly to itself in a hurt sort of way.

John tried to ignore his helper, but the seeds of doubt were growing. Try as he might he wasn't able to dismiss the sulking computer from his mind.

"Well? You disbelieving box! Come straight out with it. What would you do in the circumstances?"

"I would wait a few days to check that we really have succeeded, master. Two more days will not make much difference, if you intend to live forever."

"Hm! You don't think I can do it, do you? If that's what you advise I'll be patient and wait a few days. But, mark my words, it'll make no difference. You seem very cautious: that's what you suggested at the Hall Gardens; pick some and wait and see, you said. In a day or two when these beauties are still unwrinkled and pristine, you will have to admit I was right."

Tactfully, Omni kept its opinions to itself.

In town, at the vegetable show, Roger insisted that Oswald should leave the show and return with him to the pharmacy, where Malcolm and a Saturday girl were coping on their own. He wanted to share his good news with the Chemist and was feeling a bit guilty at taking the whole day off.

97

Oswald was already in a happy mood from the beer, and readily agreed to accompany the lad to tell his twin brother of their success.

"I've won the silver cup for the best tomatoes," Roger gushed as soon as he stepped into the shop.

"Congratulations, lad." Malcolm beamed his approval. "I always knew you could do it. What will you do with all the prize money?"

Oswald sobered up as soon as he heard this comment. He hadn't considered the possibility of prize money as well as a trophy.

"How much has he won?"

"Fifty pounds is the usual amount."

Roger kissed the Saturday girl and danced excitedly along the shop floor. Oswald plotted how much rent he could charge the lad for the use of his greenhouse and garden. Malcolm smiled like a benign Toby Jug and voiced his thoughts.

"It's a pity you didn't save your fruit for the next show. There is a purse of £100 to be won at that one."

Oswald winced. All that tax-free dough going for the asking. What a waste! He set his devious mind to scheming how Roger could win the next show and how he could get his hands on a share of the loot.

Chapter Eighteen

Roger had never before been invited to Oswald's home for tea. On Saturday evening, after the show, he put on his best suit and took along the twenty winning tomatoes, as requested.

"Come in lad." The Druggist met him at the front door and ushered him into the dining room.

Roger had been looking after the garden for several months but this was the first time he had set foot inside the house. It wasn't that his employer was too stuck up to entertain staff or that he found the lad uninteresting company but the effort of clearing up the house to make it presentable was usually too much for him.

"I've brought the tomatoes, as you told me, Mr Oswald."

"Put them in the kitchen, lad."

"Shall I slice them for tea?"

Oswald shot in from the hall, his eyes ablaze with fear. "No! No thank you," he shouted. "We've a Chinese takeaway for tea."

Roger left the bag of tomatoes on the side. Oswald put them carefully into his fridge.

"Sit down Roger. We'll eat first, then I have an idea I want to discuss with you."

They ate in silence, the trainee a little overawed by the circumstances. At last, the final mouthful eaten, he asked. "Do you think I did well today, winning the silver cup, Mr Gotobed?"

"Marvellous, Roger. Even with my expert knowledge, I would be hard pressed to do better myself." Oswald was too lazy to cultivate the soil but like most armchair gardeners he was a self confessed expert on the subject.

The trainee sat at the dining table in silence, letting his eyes wander around the room, curious about the Druggist's home, for he had heard all the rumours about magic and the supernatural. His mother had pooh-poohed the idea, saying that the RUFS were only some harmless male, secret society like the Boy Scouts, the Freemasons or the Ku-Klux-Clan. Roger was not so sure, he had overheard customers asking Mr Gotobed to conjure up fine weather, make sure a certain horse won at the races, or supply a love potion.

"Enjoying yourself?" Oswald asked in an avuncular way. Most unusually, he oozed charm. This put the lad on edge.

"I mustn't be too late home. My mum is expecting me soon."

"Don't worry, Roger. I only want to help you make some more money from your gardening exploits."

The lad fidgeted even more. He knew Oswald's reputation where money was concerned.

"Wouldn't it be marvellous if you could win the tomato class at the next show in two weeks time."

"I haven't any more fruit left. There was only one plant in the first place."

"I know. But what if your winning crop was to keep in perfect condition for the next two weeks? You could show them and win again. Only next time there is a hundred pounds prize money."

"If only." Roger fancied a new mountain bike. If only it was that easy, he thought.

"I have some expertise in keeping things fresh," the High Wizard volunteered.

"I don't think your fridge or the preservative you use in the medicines and eye-drops will stop my fruit from rotting. Will they, Mr Gotobed?"

"That's not exactly what I had in mind. You may have heard that I have been researching Time Magic in the cellar workshop and at the RUFS. I have had some small successes."

Roger shifted uncomfortably in his chair. Talk of magic and all that stuff made him feel nervous. It was OK in storybooks or even on TV, but in real life he felt these things should not happen.

"Now I must discuss with you the rent you owe for the use of the garden." Oswald suddenly changed tack in his efforts to persuade the lad to co-operate.

"Rent?"

"Nothing too much, lad. Say fifty pounds for the whole season."

Roger coloured up bright red. Five pounds was out of the question, let alone fifty!

"There's no way I can pay you that amount, Mr Gotobed," he said in dismay, praying the Druggist wouldn't stop it out of his wages.

"Oh, but there is, Roger. You could win twice that amount with your prize tomatoes. Just let me put the fluence on them to keep them fresh, then enter them in the next show under your name, exactly as you did this time."

"You could enter them yourself, Mr Oswald."

Oswald had already considered this option but with Peele being secretary to the RUFS as well as the Allotment Holders' Association, his magic capabilities were too well known to get away with that ruse. Anyway, everybody knew he loathed gardening.

"That would hardly be fair, Roger. You have done all the work, you should get all the credit. All I want is half the prize money for letting you use my facilities and maybe the rosette to paste in my scrapbook. It's a straight forward enough business arrangement, surely?"

"Oh alright then. What do I have to do?"

Oswald sighed with relief. He thought the lad was going to be difficult, or maybe even threaten to mention his plan to Malcolm. That would never do.

"Enter your tomatoes as you did last time. I will keep them here in my fridge until the day of the show. You just do exactly as you did before."

"I might not win, you understand. Mr Clay would have beaten me last time if someone hadn't stolen his entry." The boy coloured up again; the thought had just struck him that maybe Oswald had stolen Clay's prize tomatoes. But he realised the Druggist had been hardly sober enough for such tricks. The only person he had noticed was that strange, military looking gentleman who had called in the shop for two aspirins.

"We'll have to do what we can about Mr Clay." Oswald said under his breath. But it was more out of bravado than any definite plan he had in mind.

"I'll have to go, Mr Gotobed. You do what you like with my tomatoes. Eat them if you like, I don't mind. But as you insist, I'll put my name down for the next show."

"Good lad. Give my regards to your mother and mind how you go on your way home."

Roger left with a sigh of relief. Mr Oswald could be a funny old beggar at times, especially when he got a bee in his bonnet about something.

Once the lad had left, the High Wizard took the tomatoes from the fridge and set them on his dining table. They still looked as good as they had at the show, thank goodness he had caught them in time.

He made the necessary magic passes over them and recited a Latin spell. By the time he replaced them in the refrigerator the fruit were in a state of suspended animation; the natural ripening and rotting processes had been postponed for several weeks. He had every confidence in his ability to stave off the onset of old age in the tomatoes, at least until after the next show. If they rotted rapidly after that it wouldn't matter. Now he must give some thought to spoiling Greenfingers' chances of competing.

Chapter Nineteen.

Omni had been right, all along. Two days after the vegetable show the stolen tomatoes were showing signs of ageing; the process accelerated by the warmth of the hotel bedroom. Their skins were wrinkled and sagging, they had turned from a healthy orange to an over-ripe crimson and their youthful firmness had given way to a soft squidginess. John Buttadaeus, being 180 years old himself, and very aware of his advancing age, recognised the signs all too well.

"You were right for once," he growled at his black box. "I cannot understand how we stole the winning fruit but did not get the everlasting sample."

"You broke the cardinal rule of time travel, master."

John glared at his computer. "What are you going on about?"

"It is a recognised axiom when time travelling, as you well know. Never alter anything in the past or you may upset the future."

The time traveller lay back above his bed preparing himself for a long lecture from his box. He could have switched the know-all off, but he knew all too well that Omni was right.

"The classical example is a time traveller who goes into his own past and accidentally kills his own grandfather before his own father is conceived. You know full well this would alter the traveller's future and he could no longer be born. That silly accident would ensure he had no future and he would cease to exist."

"So what?" John growled uneasily.

"You removed the tomatoes that were going to win the first prize and in so doing altered history. Presumably the second best fruit won the prize and everything is now different."

John sat up abruptly, wagging his finger at the black box. "Retrieve that newspaper report once again and see if the past is now reported differently."

Omni buzzed busily and checked the report of the vegetable show. "No. No change to the news report. Nothing has altered. It still states that everlasting tomatoes won the Runford vegetable show in August 1996. That means..."

"How can that be? We know Clay's tomatoes would have won and we know I have them on my bedside cabinet, all mushy and useless, with blue fungi growing on them."

Omni was about to try and explain, when his master lost patience and clicked the computer off with an impatient flick of his fingers.

"I must have taken the wrong sample. Clay must have brought the wrong fruit to the show," John muttered angrily to himself as he paced up and down the bedroom carpet. "There is no choice left to me now. I must go back to the Hall garden and search for the real, everlasting fruit."

Omni, switched off in mid sentence, lay on the bedside table fuming silently. It had worked out exactly what had happened, there could only be one logical explanation. But its master wouldn't listen. If that's the way he wants it, then he can manage without me, it thought huffily. Its circuits and microchips bristled with indignation.

John hovered just above his bed and rested, making his plans. The first thing he would need was a place to hide the stolen fruit, for there would be a lot of it.

He had noticed a card in the antique shop window, advertising a cottage to rent. He called at Willis' antique shop.

"That card in your window. The cottage, can I rent it?"

Theo looked up from the desk where he was busy ageing modern photocopies of antique maps in a tray of cold tea, and shouted to his wife. "Some bloke after your holiday cottage. Can you come and deal with him please."

Dora Willis had been left a small riverside cottage in her mother's will. Instead of selling it, she decided to rent it out to holidaymakers and fishermen. The income was useful because her husband was mean with the housekeeping and there was always the thought that she would have somewhere to live if her life with Theo at Church House became intolerable.

"How long would you like it for?"

"Just a week." John held out a wad of coffee stained ten-pound notes and smiled.

"Right, here's the key. If you wait a minute, I'll take you down to the cottage and show you round." Mrs Willis counted out her rent, handed him his depleted roll of notes and put on her coat.

Honeysuckle cottage was down a secluded lane, by the river.

"Ideal, this is." The stranger clicked his heels, took her hand in his and kissed it curtly.

She giggled, embarrassed by his old-world charm. It was a pity her husband never behaved like that towards her; such manners made her feel attractive. Still glowing from the compliment, she opened the cottage.

"Kitchen and lounge, downstairs; bathroom and two bedrooms above. There's a log store out in the yard and an open fire in the sitting room. It's a warm little house. You'll probably not need to light the fire."

"Dear Lady. Indebted to you I am most awfully." He saw her to the door and gave her a little wave when she turned to look back.

When she was out of sight he clapped his hands with glee. He looked out of the lounge window over the river and congratulated himself on acquiring such an ideal hideout.

"Phase one of my master plan completed. I now have the premises and they are most private."

As dusk fell John Buttadaeus locked his new-found home and walked out of the town, passing by the Dog in a Doublet with its coloured light bulbs illuminating the car park. He intended to go to the Hall that same evening but first he needed substantial transport for his plans.

At the council depot the dustmen had completed their last round and gone home, or to the pub. Only the driver was working late, hosing out his dustcart to prepare it for the next day's work. He heard the crunch of feet on gravel as someone crossed the yard. Looking over his shoulder, he recognised the new arrival as the man who had asked him directions at the Hall.

" 'ello again. What can we do for you, mate?"

John smiled reassuringly, sidled up close to the man and touched him on the back of his neck. Immediately the driver dropped the pressure hose and stood still, like a zombie rooted to the spot.

"Your lorry, I need to borrow and yourself to drive it."

The dustman turned off the water tap and climbed obediently into the driving seat, moving stiffly like a mechanical man.

"To the Hall, take me."

They drove off at a steady pace, the driver staring straight ahead like a man sleep-driving with his eyes open..

At the Hall garden, John leapt down from the dustcart, unbolted the gate, and directed the vehicle into the yard. He had taken the precaution of putting Omni on guard and was ready for the Alsatian guard dog, when it appeared. One brief touch under the collar and the animal was fast asleep at his feet.

"Master! Two human life-forms coming this way."

"Whistle a tune and act as a decoy," John hissed at his little black helper.

Greenfingers Clay had been bitterly disappointed at their failure to win the tomato class at the first show and had no intention of letting anything deprive them of revenge at the next show, in a fortnight's time. The head gardener had arranged for one of them to do guard duty in the greenhouse every night, taking it in turns to sleep there. That evening Greenfingers had been checking things over and was just preparing to leave his lad on night duty when they heard a lorry backing into the garden.

"Eh up, Boss! Someone's up to no good."

"Bring that pitchfork and come with me."

Clay, looking like a member of the wartime Home Guard, crept silently towards the intruders.

Omni whistled a tune. The strains of 'Come into the garden, Maud', echoed hauntingly among the silent greenhouses and cold frames.

Clay and his helper hesitated in the half light, unable to see anyone in the dustcart's cab because John had ordered the driver to hide below the dashboard and had hidden himself behind a nearby heap of grass cuttings and horse manure.

"Where's that noise coming from?" Clay asked edgily.

"Beats me. Seems to be in the middle of the path over there."

"What's the dustcart coming for, this time of an evening. He's not due today and they never work this late," Clay grumbled as he crept towards the whistling sound. With a sigh of relief he spotted the small dark box on the pathway.

"Bless me! It's some kind of tiny transistor radio." The gardener bent over Omni and peered at it curiously. The lad lowered his fork and joined his boss, standing beside him; both their backs were turned towards the compost heap.

John moved swiftly and silently like an SAS commando and before either of the men was aware of him, he had touched them both lightly on the back of their necks and had them under his power.

"The dustcart. Back it up to that glass house," John ordered his driver. "You two. Follow me." He retrieved Omni and led the way to the main glasshouse, where the tomato crop was growing. Once the cart was in place and all three men stood statue-like before him, he issued his orders.

"Every tomato you will pick. In the back of the lorry you will place them. You will not damage the fruit. One at a time you will put them down. Silent you will be with no talking. Go to it, time there is little of."

The pressed gang toiled all through the night. Clay, the lad and the dustman picked every tomato from the plants and placed them in the back of the cart. John lounged in the driver's seat, overseeing his workers in the rear view mirror and keeping his eyes peeled for any other intruders. By four in the morning every single tomato had been picked and carefully stowed away.

"Sleep." John ordered the gardeners, then directed the driver to take his cargo back to Runford.

The town was still sleeping when the dustcart rolled through the deserted streets and down to the riverside. They backed the lorry up to the open cottage door and John ordered the driver to carefully activate the tip up mechanism. Millions of tomatoes rolled from the back of the lorry into the cottage, spreading over the living room floor and overflowing into the kitchen.

The only witnesses to these strange events were two fishermen, huddled over their rods in the grey dawn light.

"Did you see what I saw? Funny old business that."

"Can't imagine what anyone would want with millions of ripe tomatoes. Can you?"

"Must be having a large barbecue."

"Or making hundreds of gallons of ketchup."

Chapter Twenty.

Monday evening was the time for the regular monthly meeting of the RUFS. Oswald Gotobed was giving the Founder's Memorial Lecture and there was a good attendance. This was not only because the High Wizard was held in such esteem by the rank and file members, but also because of the free refreshments provided after the speech. The Dog in a Doublet outside catering department always did them proud.

As Lydia Postlethwaite marshalled her temporary staff in a side room, the lecture hall filled to capacity with the members and their guests. Among the chattering mass of regulars, one military looking stranger was hardly noticeable. Lydia had suggested John Buttadaeus might enjoy the entertainment. He, having nothing better to do than wait for a million tomatoes to mature, had taken Omni out for the evening.

"You'll enjoy the ham sandwiches," Lydia had assured him. While she was speaking he had secretly popped a meal replacement tablet in his mouth, choosing a salmon flavoured one for a change. Talk of food had whetted his appetite.

"Before we start the lecture, there are a few announcements," Oswald shouted above the din. "We have a car boot sale in aid of funds, next Sunday. Lydia has kindly allowed us to use the Dog in a Doublet car park and has promised refreshments will be on sale all day. We still need a volunteer to read the Runes in the fortune telling booth. The beginners spelling class, for newer acolytes, starts on the first Monday evening of next month.

I will be giving six lectures on self control in your sex life and its effect on your magic."

The audience gradually settled down during these preliminaries. Deciding it was time to make a start, Oswald cleared his throat and began his speech.

"The Runford Union of Fenland Slodgers, named after the old fenmen who survived by fishing and trapping wildfowl in these parts, is two hundred years old this year. Our founder, The illustrious Magus Williams, who married a faerie Princess and learned from her the secrets of faerie magic, used to deliver this lecture, until he returned to his native Black Mountains in Powys. That was many years ago, of course. Each anniversary we try to obtain the services of an expert speaker. The honour this year has fallen to me as your High Wizard to give this bicentennial lecture." Oswald cleared his throat again and gathered his notes together. "The title of this year's talk is, Oswald Gotobed's Rule of Inevitability."

"That's a big mouthful, Os," one wag shouted from the back row. "I hope the talk is shorter than the title."

Oswald ignored the banter and plunged straight into his prepared speech.

"Many of you know that I can control the weather, hence the fine days we always enjoy in Runford for our fetes and horticultural shows."

"It pays your beer money," someone sniggered loudly.

"I have been keeping records of sunlight hours and rainfall since I started dabbling in weather magic. I am amazed to report that, in spite my success, the last few years have still been average, meteorologically speaking. The rainfall and sunshine were exactly as statistics would have us expect. My tinkering with the climate had no measurable effect, yet I made fine weather when I needed it. This can only mean one thing. Nature has corrected my adjustments and inevitably things have evened out.

It seems changes brought about by magic, have a tendency to be nullified in the long run." Oswald reached for his glass of water to lubricate his dry throat.

"This initial observation led me to conduct some experiments to verify these seemingly inevitable changes. With this in mind I have called the effect my Rule of Inevitability."

By now the audience had become engrossed in the lecture. Many of the more experienced adepts nodded in agreement with Oswald's discovery. They could cite examples from their own work when this had happened. Others shook their heads in disagreement.

Oswald continued. "I know you don't want to listen to me speaking all evening..."

"You can say that again," someone heckled.

"... so, I have devised a demonstration for your education to give my voice a break."

At this juncture, a helper brought in a pint glass of Ruddles best bitter from the buffet. Oswald eyed it thirstily.

"About time too," Paddy shouted. Other regular drinkers joined in the barracking.

Oswald, ignoring his thirst and the hecklers, placed the drink under a large glass dome and called for silence.

"I have been perfecting Time Magic recently, and would like to give you a small demonstration." He put his hands around the glass dome, recited an obscure Latin spell under his breath and closed his eyes in concentration. A hush fell on the room, broken by cries of encouragement, as the spell took effect. Slowly the beer turned back to a handful of barley, a pinch of yeast, a few hops and a lot of water. Oswald held up the glass for all to see.

"Conjurer's party tricks!" John muttered to himself.

"Now I will replace the glass under the cover and carry on with my talk. I would advise you to listen to me but keep your eyes on the beer glass."

The Wizard droned on with numerous other examples of his observations, finishing up with the parable of his individual fruit pie.

The audience watched the beer glass intently. Gradually, one then another of them pointed at the transparent dome and turned to his neighbour to check that they were seeing the same things. The raw ingredients of the drink appeared to be recombining to form beer again. When the process was complete Oswald stopped and lifted off the cover. A rancid smell filled the room!

"Cor! That Bitter is off!" The cry rose from several expert lips.

"Quite so." Oswald agreed, rapidly taking in the situation. "The beer has reformed, but not quite in the same way. Left to their own devices the hops and barley have returned to their brewed state. I am not sure why the beer is no longer drinkable, but it seems the magic energy used has somehow upset the equation. It is a salutary lesson for all wizards. Do not frivolously use your powers for they will inevitably be reversed and sometimes with adverse effects."

The audience applauded, especially when the High Wizard replaced the airtight cover over the rancid beer. Oswald held up his hand for one last silence.

"I am supported in my research by the work of the illustrious, Sir Isaac Newton. He was another learned Lincolnshire scientist, who dabbled in alchemy and the occult. Sir Isaac gave us his famous Laws of Motion. His third Law of Motion states, 'to every action there is an opposite and equal reaction.' At present my research is at an early stage and I am finding the Rule can sometimes be broken. When I have understood these anomalies I may change the title to Oswald Gotobed's LAW of Inevitability." The Wizard drew himself up to his full five foot three and grasped his lapels with his fingertips. "I rest my case."

Everyone clapped madly. Some of the more experienced members understood it but the newer ones were just relieved it was time to sample the buffet. John Buttadaeus smiled to himself. He had expected no better of primitive scientists from the twentieth century. Magic! He nearly laughed aloud. Omni kept silent, the miniature computer knew better.

"Before we start to eat." Oswald's voice was drowned in the protest. He banged his fist on the lectern, demanding silence once more. "One more announcement that I forgot at the beginning. Our secretary, police sgt Peele, who is also secretary to the Allotment Holders Association, has asked me to remind you that their annual show will be held as usual in the park, one week on Saturday. All you gardeners had better get your exhibits ready."

Deep inside John Buttadaeus' pocket, Omni buzzed excitedly to itself.

Chapter Twenty One

Before he made his way home to the Dog in a Doublet, John Buttadaeus called at the cottage he had rented from Mrs Willis. He pushed open the door, forcing hundreds of tomatoes along the linoleum, squashing many of them against the walls. He noticed a different smell about the place. Several million ordinary tomatoes trapped in a warm room, those near the bottom bearing the weight of the countless thousands above them, soon develop a characteristic smell. It is the unmistakable odour of decay!

"Phew! What's that smell, Omni?"

"Could it possibly be rotting fruit?"

"Damnation! Will I have to sort out the few everlasting ones from this decaying mass?"

"I think perhaps non of these tomatoes is immortal, master. We have made a terrible mistake."

John turned on his black box in temper and was about to inflict some awful revenge on it when a light knock came at the front door.

"Whose that?"

"Dora Willis, your landlady. I've just called round, to see if there's anything you wanted. I hope everything is satisfactory, Mr Buttadaeus. I hope you've settled in alright." The lady had found herself at a loose end that evening. Remembering her lodger's attentive charm, she had tidied herself up, taken a walk and found herself drifting in the direction of Honeysuckle cottage.

John skulked behind the cottage door, up to his knees in squashed tomatoes. His socks and trousers were speckled with the seeds and juice from the damaged fruit. The odour of fungi and decaying vegetation filled his nostrils and there was a sea of bubbling juice with bobbing red spheres and slimy skins floating all around him.

"Everything is fine, Mrs Willis. In fact it couldn't be better."

Omni buzzed audibly.

"Keep your robot mouth shut and I'll forgive you," John hissed urgently in the box's artificial ear hole.

Mrs Willis waited some minutes at the door, not sure if she was to be invited in or whether she should go. Luckily, she didn't notice the orange juice and yellow seeds oozing under the door.

"Tell her you can't ask her in. Tell her you're getting ready for bed. Explain to her you are feeling tired from travelling." Omni whispered.

John repeated the excuses aloud. After a few minutes of silence, he was relieved to hear her footsteps retreating up the driveway away from the cottage.

"What am I to do now? How are we to clear up this mess?" John asked his black box in despair. "I can't let that lady see her home in this state. She reminds me too much of my mother, when I was a boy."

"I would suggest we find some people to help us, just as you did when we transported the fruit here. If you wait until nightfall there will be some more of those strange men with sticks, string and feather floats, sitting by the riverside."

John squelched his way upstairs and washed his socks and trousers under the bath taps. This whole business was becoming a nightmare to him, yet he still clung stubbornly to his hopes. He still felt the chance of everlasting life was worth all the effort and problems.

117

Omni cleared its electronic throat and spoke. "I detect three humans wearing anoraks. They will be bird watchers, train spotters or fishermen. As it is now dark, there are no railway lines nearby and they have live worm life-forms in their pockets, I deduce it's the last possibility. They must be fisherman."

The old man lowered himself out of the cottage window and crept stealthily up on the trio. The three lads were submerging a pack of beer cans in a keep net to keep it cool, and preparing for a night's fishing at the waterside. Hiding in the rushes, John waited until they were completely engrossed in their hobby; mesmerised by the drifting reflection of the full moon on the water surface and lulled almost to sleep by the gentle lapping of the waves at the water's edge. The fact that the fish were not biting, made them even more sleepy.

John sneaked up on them, one by one, and subdued them with his neck grip. "Follow me." He ordered, once he had sorted out the last man.

The three rose from their deckchairs without question, and shuffled after him in the moonlight to the cottage, where he set them to work on his stolen tomatoes.

The task took them most of the night. They worked as a human chain to sort out the mass of rotting fruit, passing each tomato in front of Omni's all seeing eye, for it to check the genetic makeup of each one, searching for the everlasting examples. By dawn the cottage was completely empty of tomatoes. They had discovered not a single pristine example and had thrown all the red fruit through the window into the river, where it bobbed up and down on the tide like some gigantic game of water snooker.

John looked around the downstairs rooms and realised he could not leave them in such a filthy state. He armed his work crew with mops, sponges, towels and buckets and made them clean up the mess, drying out the walls and floors with a hair drier and a crackling log fire.

Each one worked like Hercules cleaning out the Aegian Stables.

John actually felt almost sorry for them, and by way of compensation, pushed a couple of ten pound notes into each of their anoraks before he let them go.

By seven in the morning the fishermen were back on the riverbank, totally unaware of why they felt so tired, wondering why the beer cans were still unopened, and amazed they had caught no fish. All three were oblivious to the tomato juice drying on their clothing. They packed up at eight in the morning, disappointed with their night's sport.

On their way home, the three men were stopped by a policeman, who enquired if they had noticed anything strange in the night.

"What exactly could we have seen constable?"

"We suspect the canning factory has been tipping a bad batch of Tomato Soup into the river, turning it into a mini version of the Red Sea and polluting the waterway. Did you hear anything or see anyone doing that along the river, boys?"

"We saw nothing, constable," they chorused.

"Ah well...By the way, did you catch anything?"

One of the lads opened up his bag to reveal several kilos of squashed tomatoes! They were detained all morning at the police station, as they tried to explain how they came to have the fruit. Grudgingly the duty constable eventually accepted their story and was about to let them put on their anoraks and go, when sergeant Peele decided to search them. He noticed the ten pound notes in their pockets.

"Can we go now, Sergeant Peele? We've told you all we know about the tomatoes"

"Aye lad, you told us all about the tomatoes. But what about the forged ten pound notes in your pockets?"

"Ten-pound notes! What ten-pound notes?"

The duty sergeant spread six, coffee stained notes on his desk top.

"They look genuine enough to me, Serg," the constable ventured.

"Too right they do. They are bloody marvellous forgeries. The paper's right. The ink is correct, even when viewed under the Ultra Violet light. There's a metal strip and a watermark in them. Every single one is perfect. In fact, seen singly you wouldn't suspect a thing."

"So, what's the problem?"

"They're all the same number!" Sgt Peele answered triumphantly.

"Good Lord! What do we do now?"

"Get a warning circulated to the local banks and the Chamber of Trade. Take these suspects through to the cells and get a written statement from them. We may have an epidemic of crime on our hands."

Back at his lodgings at Lydia's hostelry, John lay soaking in a hot bath, trying to remove the smell of rotten tomatoes from his body. The aroma of hot fruit drifted down the stairs and filled the bar. Omni lay on the chair under a bath towel. The robot cleared its artificial throat as if it intended to speak.

"Well, Omni. What now?" John sighed.

"I think we have made a mistake with the date of the vegetable show, master."

"How come?" John disengaged his big toe from the hot tap, pulled the towel off the chair, and paid full attention to his computer.

"This evening, in that lecture, Mr Gotobed mentioned the Allotment Holders' Show in one weeks time. Could that be the show we are looking for? It's still in the month of August in the year 1996. It would also fit the description in the news item."

"You're a genius, Omni!"

"No, you're the genius, master. Your IQ is only 180!"

John glanced sideways at the box, but swallowed his anger and smiled. He felt he could put up with its mechanical arrogance if it got him what he wanted.

"What would I do without you, Omni. You must be the cleverest thing in the universe."

Omni wasn't fooled. It is difficult to pull the wool over the eyes of a computer with an artificial IQ of over 500.

Chapter Twenty Two.

The telephone at the Hall gardens rang out shrilly through the early morning mist. Greenfingers Clay, who'd spent the night guarding his greenhouses, stretched himself and yawned before he went to his office to answer the call from his wife.

"No dear. We've had no more trouble, just a couple of tomcats upset the guard dog at two in the morning but nothing more exciting than that. I had to tether the damn dog over near the house to get some peace." He lit the paraffin stove to boil the water for his first coffee of the day and unlocked the gate for the lad to get in. Since that awful night when all his prize tomatoes had mysteriously vanished he had insisted he and the trainee took it in turns to do armed, guard duty each night. The lad thought it was closing the greenhouse door after the tomatoes had bolted, but Clay was a stubborn man and the sense of violation he felt at losing his beloved crop was still fresh in his mind. The fact that he and the lad had both been on duty when the theft had taken place, but neither of them remembered hearing a thing, had left him guilt ridden and determined to make amends.

The boy wheeled his cycle into the garden, a black plastic refuse sack balanced on his handlebars.

"I've got another one, Mr Clay. I found it in a derelict glasshouse on a disused allotment. Nobody will miss it."

"Bring it in here, where nobody can see us." Clay beckoned the lad into the potting shed.

"That's six in all, with the five I took from that empty house on the Wash Road."

Clay took a folded fiver from his back pocket and pushed it into the lad's grateful hand.

"Allicanti; a good variety of tomato that. Looks as if it needs some feed and tender loving care, but it's definitely got possibilities." The gardener scrutinised his new plant like a racehorse trainer checking over a new addition to his string of horses. "We'd better plant it next to the other five, just inside the doorway of the glasshouse, where we can keep a eye on them."

Slowly and secretly, Clay was building up a small stock of fruiting tomato plants. It was much too late in the year to sow seeds again and he knew he couldn't ask any of his rivals for help, they wouldn't even give him the time of day, so he paid the lad to keep his eyes open for any plants going spare. Greenfingers was set on entering the Allotment holders' show and winning back his self-respect by taking first place with the best tomatoes in the fens. Granted the stock they had purloined was not the most promising material, not being the progeny of his own cross pollination programme, but it was amazing what good husbandry could achieve and he still had a trick or two up his manure stained sleeves.

Clay's self satisfaction was shattered later that morning when the secretary from the Hall announced a lightning visit was due from the boss. The Member for the fens and two of his parliamentary mates were scheduled to inspect the garden the very next day, after a constituency meeting at the town hall and a slap up lunch at the best hotel.

"Damn and blast the man!" Greenfingers cursed as soon as the girl was out of earshot. "He brings his cronies down to my garden just to impress them and brag how HIS tomatoes will win the silver cup and how HIS runner beans, I mean French beans now he's gone pro Common Market, are the biggest in the county.

123

Why can't he leave us to the proper work while he plays at governing the country?"

With that initial outburst over, the gardener had to face up to some pressing problems. How could he pass six assorted stolen plants off as a whole greenhouse full of prize tomatoes? Even if his boss bothered to step just inside the doorway of the glasshouse, one glance would tell him there was something very wrong.

"You can't help it if thieves stole the crop, Mr Clay," the boy sympathised.

"It's all very well you saying that, lad, but that's not how he'll see it. He'll say I should have tightened security. He'll question our need for a guard dog and even why I employ you, if I can't keep track of my produce. It's just the kind of thing those Members of Parliament have already done to the schools and the hospitals; cut back staff, cut back resources and expect miracles. This needs some thinking about. I'll have another coffee then we'll plan what we'll do."

Clay was nothing if not imaginative. He hatched a plan that he thought had a slim chance of success, if the light was bad and the visitors had too much after dinner Port before the visit. As he told his apprentice. "We ain't no choice. Beggars can't be choosers. The show's not over till the fat lady sings."

The gardener's plan was simple. They would convince any casual observer that the glasshouse was still full to the eves with first class ripe tomatoes. His original vines were still in place, standing bare in sad rows along the length of the glasshouse like forlorn skeletons. He had not dug them out and they were exactly as the tomato thieves had left them; plenty of healthy stems, a few leaves, but not one solitary fruit.

"Go up to the Hall and ask the secretary for the box of glass baubles they use to decorate the giant spruce we put in the hallway each Christmas."

The lad scampered off, soon returning heavily laden.

He was not given a chance to waste time.

"Go into Runford and buy all the sound tomatoes the greengrocer will sell you. Try and get orange ones; we don't want them too ripe, otherwise they'll not keep. We'll attach them to the empty vines. Pick up twelve tubes of that there Superior Glue." Clay ordered, as soon as the lad had struggled back to the potting shed and unloaded the huge box of Christmas decorations. "By the way, did she ask why you needed the baubles?"

" 'fraid so, Mr Clay."

"What did you tell her?"

"It was your wife's birthday and you wanted to give her a surprise party."

"Good thinking, but don't tell my wife."

When his helper had set out for town on his bicycle, dragging the garden wheelbarrow clanking behind him, the head gardener set to decorating the glasshouse. He chose to work on the bare tomato plants furthest from the door; the ones which had been stripped of all their crop under John Buttadaeus influence. Clay selected only the green, yellow and red glass balls and twisted a few onto each forlorn stem. He knew real tomato plants would have green unripe fruit, yellowish ones, which were beginning to ripen, and red tomatoes ready for picking. By half closing his eyes and looking into the sunlight he kidded himself the coloured glass baubles would just pass for his lost crop.

In Runford the lad visited the greengrocers.

"How many did you say?" The assistant asked incredulously.

"As many as you will sell me," the gardener repeated quietly.

"I've five trays out the back, but they've got to last us until the weekend. Don't you have any tomatoes up at the Hall?"

"It's nothing to do with the Hall," the lad lied hastily. "It's me mother. She likes tomato chutney."

The greengrocer scratched his head. Usually they used green tomatoes to make chutney. Perhaps this was some new craze. He made a note to ask his wife to check with the WI next time she went to a meeting.

The ironmongers were equally cautious in selling him twelve tubes of Superiorglue. They had been warned by the police, that practical jokers had been smearing the seats of the public lavatories with the gel and some stupid yobbos had even tried sniffing the product. The casualty staff at the cottage hospital, were fed up removing the tubes from young lads' noses and prising toilet seats from ladies bottoms.

"What do you need twelve tubes for? You're not breaking the law, are you?"

"Me dad makes models. He's working on the Titanic at the moment. It's almost lifesize, it's a whopper."

"Sure his name's not Noah? Tell him to keep the windows open when he uses all this, otherwise he may be overcome with the fumes."

It was mid morning when Clay stopped for his third mug of strong coffee. He was pleased to see the lad return to the garden on his bicycle, the full barrow tethered behind it was covered over with a sack.

"Good lad! You even thought to camouflage the spoils. After lunch we'll try to glue one or two of these bought tomatoes onto each vine, using that there Superiorglue. I must make sure they look convincing, before the boss arrives.

Chapter Twenty Three

On the very evening that Clay and his helper were preparing their crop, hoping to fool the boss when he visited next day, Oswald decided to pay a secret call on the Hall garden, to gauge the strength of the opposition. He pocketed a small can of weedkiller from the shop gardening stock just in case nature needed a helping hand. Oswald strolled out of town trying to look like any other innocent country lover, enjoying an evening ramble. His route took him to the back of the Hall just as it was getting dusk. At the side gate he glanced in and saw the gardener talking to his lad in the main greenhouse. Through the shaded pains of glass he could see row upon row of laden tomato plants with perfectly formed red, yellow and green fruit dangling from them. How did these old gardeners get every fruit to be a perfect sphere and exactly the same size, he asked himself enviously? They must polish each one with a duster to get such a deep shine on it. He dodged behind a high clump of nettles as Greenfingers came through the gate. The head gardener let himself out of the garden and securely locked the gate behind him.

"See you in the morning lad. Keep alert for trouble and try not to fire that shotgun by mistake."

The Wizard cursed silently to himself. They were keeping watch over their crop and the guard was armed. They must have something very special in there, to warrant using a gun. He just had to get a look at the contents of that greenhouse.

Oswald, being High Wizard to the RUFS, was well versed in magic. Invisibility Spells were part of his repertoire. Closing his eyes he recited the appropriate Latin incantation and slowly vanished. One minute he was standing beside the red brick wall the next he was gone. He was quite good at the vanishing trick but there was one small snag; there was always some grit in Oswald's Vaseline. Almost everything became invisible; his whole body, his shirt, even his suit disappeared, but his shoes and socks remained stubbornly visible.

127

Of course the Wizard was aware of this failing and had spent countless hours pouring over grimoires, spell books and magic correspondence courses, to solve the problem, but he couldn't. An experienced older wizard he had consulted on the internet, had put it down to psychological problems. He thought Oswald must have a thing about his feet. He had asked, was the Druggist perhaps ashamed of them? Did his feet bother him? Oswald had to admit there was possibly some truth in that suggestion, for they were not a pretty sight, with corns, bunions and ingrowing toenails. He was not fond of anyone seeing them, he even kept his socks on when he made love, but then everyone he'd ever seen in the Blue Movies seemed to do the same, so that didn't bother him too much. As the Wizard could not overcome the problem, he had came to terms with it; removing his socks and shoes whenever he used the invisibility spell. He took off his shoes and socks and climbed the garden gate, completely unseen because he was bare footed.

Inside the garden, Greenfingers Clay ran an organic regime. No chemical slug killer, fungicides or DDT sprays for him. He used the old and tried methods; spreading eggshells and sharp grit to keep away the snails and slugs. It worked for bare foot Wizards as well.

"Hell's bells! Who's left tin tacks all over the path?" Oswald exclaimed loudly.

"Is that you, Mr Clay? Have you forgotten something?" The boy called nervously from the glasshouse doorway, his shot gun held at the ready, an itchy index finger sweating on the trigger.

The invisible Wizard held his breath, stood perfectly still in spite of the searing pain in the sole of his right foot. Gradually the emergency passed and the under gardener returned to his deck chair and his girly magazine. Oswald, balanced on one leg in the middle of the path like some grotesque, transparent, garden gnome, breathed a sigh of relief and looked around for somewhere safe to place his next step.

He was in luck. Just inside the gate he spied a pair of size twelve Wellington boots, left there by Greenfingers on his way home.

Inside the glasshouse, the lad was reading by the light of an oil lamp, occasionally swatting the gnats attracted by the pool of golden brightness. He was a nervous youth, glancing uneasily about the glasshouse, imagining all sorts of monsters and ghouls hidden in the shadows of the lank plants. He had to admit in this light their mock-up of a healthy crop looked convincing. By the door, where the casual observer would first look, they had planted the real fruit-bearing plants he had stolen. Next along the row was the greengrocers' contribution; all the bought tomatoes suspended on the vine by Superiorglue. They had only just completed this part of the operation when Mr Clay decided to go home for his supper. In the far reaches of the greenhouse the bare plants with Christmas baubles twisted onto them, stood in gleaming rows. Each red, yellow and green orb reflecting the yellow lantern light with a bright spot of gilded highlight. Those are not too convincing, in this light, the lad conceded, but perhaps in daylight they wouldn't be so obvious, especially if he turned on the mist sprayer as the visitors arrived, just as Mr Clay had suggested.

Oswald crept towards the lighted greenhouse, pausing at every step so that a casual observer would just believe someone had carelessly left a pair of Wellies on the path. He stepped silently over the threshold of the tomato house and froze into immobility as the lad glanced up nervously from his magazine. Endless minutes of tense waiting were rewarded when the youthful guard returned to his centrefold, tilting the book upside down to get a different slant on the nude Pet of the Month.

"Dirty little sod! You'll go blind." Oswald whispered. The lad looked up nervously, saw nothing unusual, and put the faint sound down to the wind outside. He grunted as he noticed that his boss had left his rubber boots in the doorway.

"Uh! That's not like him. He usually leaves 'em by the gate. I'll take 'em to the potting shed when I make me next coffee."

Oswald was engrossed in the tomato crop by the doorway. Not a very good crop for Greenfingers, he thought, not at all the class of fruit he usually shows. Perhaps he's kept the best ones further in the greenhouse; away from the draughts, the direct sunlight and the occasional visitor with light fingers. Maybe these are for eating? The Wizard dragged his heavy boots along the dusty earth floor, trying to progress without any obvious movement, in case the boy noticed something out of the corner of his eyes.

All went to plan until Oswald reached the seventh plant in the row; this was the first of the bare vines and the last one to be adorned with bought fruit. He fingered a red tomato, trying to gauge its ripeness and how it would look on the show day. Unfortunately there was still a speck of wet Superiorglue on the green stalk. No matter how hard he pulled, the Wizard could not remove the plant from his fingers. He shook his hand, gently at first, but as he lost his patience he struggled harder, and pulled the complete vine out of the ground.

The commotion caused the under gardener to look up from his centrefold. The sight that met the lad's eyes made his young mouth gape open with fear. Along the path he saw one of the plants writhing and dancing in the air. It was swearing loudly and wearing Wellington boots, which it clumped up and down in some weird sort of tribal dance. The lad took fright. His hair stood on end. "It's the Day of the Triffids, but for real!" He yelled.

Oswald shook his hands vigorously, trapped by his fingers on the glue as securely as a Bluebottle caught on a sticky flypaper. The more he struggled the deeper he became enmeshed. He panicked, forgot the secrecy, and threw caution to the wind. "Get off my fingers you bloodsucking vampire!" He shouted fearfully.

The lad, catching the mention of bloodsucking vampires, threw down his magazine and backed away from the apparition, all lustful thoughts driven out of his mind by the desire to save his skin. He knew Mr Clay talked to the plants and sometimes treated them with as much tender loving care as he would a favourite pet, but tomato plants answering back and jumping up and down? This was too much! He turned to escape, fell over his deckchair and dropped the loaded shotgun.

Oswald was losing the struggle with the sticky vine, which had attached itself to several parts of his invisible person. He kicked out in his oversized rubber boots and tripped himself up, falling to the ground in a tangle of stems, leaves and ripe tomatoes. This was a happy accident, for at that precise moment the loaded shotgun hit the ground. The safety catch was not on. The gun went off!

Everything seemed to happen at once. There was a loud explosion. The boy took fright and jumped through the side of the glasshouse, sending glass splinters in all directions. Miraculously he was unscathed as he ran blindly for the gate and the open road. Oswald missed the worst of the blast, getting just two pellets in his bottom as he lay helpless on the earth floor. His struggles only made matters worse, as he squirmed like some defeated gladiator caught in a green net.

The healthy tomato plants by the door took the full force of the bird-shot. They were blown away. Every stem, every leaf and each fruit, shattered into a thousand fragments and spread all over the garden. All hope of a class-winning crop was gone. Greenfingers Clay had wasted his money. He might as well have pushed his fiver through the garden shredder.

Oswald, frightened to death by the noise of the explosion and stung into action by the pellets in his rear end, sprang up from the path and bolted outside, barefoot into the yard. Luckily the blast had released the plant from his fingers, but unfortunately the explosion had alerted the Alsatian guard dog who was still tethered in the far corner of the garden.

The first Oswald knew of the dog was when it raced towards him, snarling viciously with teeth dripping saliva and lips curled back from its flashing canines, a length of snapped rope flying out behind it. Faced with this fearful sight, the Wizard forgot he was invisible and ran for the gate, giving the sharp-eared dog a clue to his whereabouts.

Greenfingers Clay had just reached the main road when he heard the distant crack of a shotgun. He turned on the spot and rushed back to his garden, breaking the Olympic sprint cycle record in his haste. Those beggars weren't going to steal his crops again, and of course, he was a little concerned for the lad's safety. He threw his cycle into the ditch and vaulted the gate, landing on top of the growling Alsatian.

Oswald froze on the spot, realising the sound of his movements had given away his whereabouts to the dog. Slowly he edged towards the gate inch by invisible inch, ignoring the pain in his feet, inflicted by the sharp eggshells. The dog recovered from Clay's sudden arrival and snarled in the general direction of the invisible man. It had detected his scent but couldn't reconcile that smell with the evidence of its eyes. Suddenly a twig cracked beneath Oswald bare foot. The dog jumped towards the sound, ears back, teeth bared.

The Wizard grabbed an old fork handle from the ground and tried to ward the animal off with it. The dog closed its teeth around the stick and shook it madly.

"You stupid dog," Clay exclaimed! "What's the good of taking it out on my fork handle?" He slapped the animal across its back and shouted for it to stop. Oswald vaulted the gate in the confusion, landing barefoot in the bed of stinging nettles.

Later, at home, the Wizard spent several painful hours perched over a mirror, removing lead shot from his bottom. In bed that night he had a sleepless night, his ankles stinging and swollen from the nettle stings, his feet throbbing from the sharp, slug deterrent and his cheeks on fire from the iodine he applied to the pellet holes.

Laying on his stomach with his legs hanging over the end of the bed he had ample time to consider his night's work. At least he now knew that the Hall gardens were no threat to his plans for Roger to win at the show. All Greenfingers Clay had was a collection of out of season Christmas trees, some bare plants with fruit superglued to them, and a few real tomato plants blown far and wide in small fragments.

Chapter Twenty Four.

Frank Hogg desperately wanted to make things right with his wife. He was lonely and hungry, fending for himself. She was still staying at the women's refuge in the town, refusing to speak to him on the telephone and letting Gabby do all the talking on the doorstep, when he called on them.

It was no good thinking of solving things by travelling back in time again on the Time Machine, hoping to do better than his last attempt, for someone had stolen the brass levers that worked the thing. He'd found that out the last time he'd tried to use it. He racked his brains for a solution and in desperation asked for advice from his mates at the weekly get together of the South Linc's Chapter of the Hell's Angels at the local pub.

"Go and drag her out," one young tough suggested. "Treat her like a cave man. Women love that kind of thing." He was only a teenager and still sporting 'L' plates.

Older, wiser members of the Chapter shook their heads, drawing in their breath sharply at the suggestion. They knew men who had tried it and finished up begging on their knees at the women's refuge.

"Treat her to something nice," one of the few lady members counselled him.

He liked the sound of that, it fitted in more with his gentle temperament.

"What would you like me to buy you…if I was your man?" He added the last five words hastily, seeing her eyes light up and not wishing to be misconstrued.

"A silver ring for me bellybutton." She yanked her teashirt up and her leather jeans down and showed him her neatly pierced umbilicus with a circle of tattooed petals surrounding it. "Of course I could do with a tattoo on my bum." She started to peel down her trousers but her boyfriend put a restraining hand on her belt.

"A set of them there battery operated rollers for me hair. This bloody crash hat ruins me perm," blonde haired Samantha suggested, peeling a damp curl from her sweaty head to illustrate the problem.

Suggestions came thick and fast; the beer had loosened everybody's tongue. Unfortunately it had ruined their judgement. Frank was getting nowhere.

Lydia took pity on him, leaned over the bar and whispered in his silver ringed ear. "She'd enjoy a holiday, Frank. When did you last go away together?"

The landlady's suggestion immediately took his fancy. Freda and he had not had a holiday since their honeymoon at the motorbike rally in Wales. That was at least ten years ago. All he needed to do was to raise some cash and buy two tickets for somewhere exciting.

Back at his workshop Frank searched the back pages of his newspaper for exotic locations. He found several places he fancied but at prices he couldn't afford. He must find something of value to sell or pawn. His motorbike was in pieces being repaired; anyway, he needed it for transport, so that was out of the question. There were no valuable clocks among the sorry collection hanging on his workshop walls; every one of them needed extensive repairs, some even needed new cuckoos. He thumbed through his beer mat collection and emptied the brandy bottle doorstop of five- pence pieces but it contained a pittance. The only thing he had of any value was his clock maker's lathe. That had cost him an arm and a leg at the local auction. It would have to go, he decided regretfully. He'd have to pawn the tools of his trade.

The clock restorer worked all night to do a temporary repair on his Harley-Davidson, then took the lathe into town to the pawnshop. The pawnbroker gave him two hundred pounds for the clock lathe, and a ticket to redeem it. Frank folded the receipt in with his lottery ticket for safe keeping and moved on to the travel agent.

Bargain breaks for two were not to be had for £200 in the height of summer, unless it was a trip to Greenland or a tour of an active volcano. He bought what he could afford and prayed Freda would like his choice.

That evening the Hells Angel had a bath, even though he was not due for one, shaved off his stubble, put on his best leathers and rode his bike into town. Nestling in his top pocket were two tickets for a three day cruise of the Irish Sea combined with a tour of the Isle of Mann motorcycle circuit. In his heart were high hopes of a reconciliation with Freda.

When Frank rode into Runford, the railway crossing gates were closed for a long, goods train to pass through.. He sat patiently, staring over the railway line at the front of the women's refuge where several of the inmates were tidying up the garden. He was too far away to recognise any of the stooping figures as they vanished and reappeared between the rolling stock, but he could tell Freda was not among them. He would have spotted her slim hips and long legs anywhere, even if he was blindfolded!

The last goods van rolled by. The gates rose into the air, letting the waiting traffic stream across. Frank put his motorbike into first gear and rolled into the Refuge yard, two cruise tickets held up in his hand in a victory sign. All the women stopped their work and eyed him warily, for many of them had partners who rode motorcycles. Gabby was helping to weed the pathway. She was using a paraffin powered, flame gun to scorch off the growth of dense brambles. As soon as she spotted the motorcyclist she recognised him. Her eyes blazed and her mouth opened in a scream.

"What the hell do you think you're doing here?"

She pointed her flame gun towards him.

No one could stop a heavy Harley-Davidson at such short notice; not even an experienced rider like Frank. He rolled towards her, one leather gloved hand held up with two tour tickets in a hollow victory salute.

"You needn't make a Vee signs at me, you dirty bastard!" Gabby shouted, and the flame gun spat a long blue tongue of fire like a plume of waste gases burning off a North Sea, oilrig.

If he hadn't been wearing his leathers and his crash helmet, Frank would have been barbecued where he sat. His protective riding gear gave him enough protection to get the bike turned around and accelerate onto the roadway. His gloved hand, which took the brunt of the flame, was smoking and blistered. The cruise tickets were charred pieces of paper; two hundred pounds gone up in smoke! The bike's yellow paintwork was smouldering and pealing. Now the whole bike needed a respray, not just the dented forks and tank.

The rest of the women advanced on him like a gang of Banshees, yelling at him, throwing the rockery, garden tools and sods of earth. He turned and fled, doing a frantic wheelie over the railway crossing.

Freda, who had been indoors when her husband arrived, stepped out of the refuge doorway just as Frank accelerated away for his life. She shouted after him but her voice was drowned by the screams for his blood. Gabby put a protective arm around her and took her back into the hostel, trying to convince her that it was all for the best and the very least the bastard deserved. Freda kept her own counsel. She knew her husband must have come for a purpose. She knew he'd never looked at another woman before, not even the young blonde Angels at the Chapter. She was beginning to have her doubts about Gabby's motives.

Chapter Twenty Five.

"You Allotment Holders are the pits! You want guaranteed fine weather but you don't want to pay for it." Oswald snapped at Sergeant Peele, honorary secretary to the Allotment Holders Association.

"I will work my weather magic, the sun will shine and your gate takings will be guaranteed. But only if you hand over that free ticket and a voucher for the beer tent."

Reluctantly the secretary dug in his pocket and gave Oswald the two tickets. His arguing hadn't worked but it had been worth a try.

"No hard feelings, Os? It was the committee who suggested I try it on. They don't realise you could make it rain just as easily as you make fine weather."

The High Wizard grinned triumphantly; he never did anything for nothing these days. It was the age of the Yuppy economy, after all.

After that small hitch, all went like clockwork with the Allotment Holders' vegetable and produce show. The day was fine, the park was crowded and the different classes attracted fierce competition; with one notable exception. The class for the best tomatoes was missing its best grower. Greenfingers Clay had failed to exhibit for the first time in living memory. Roger entered the same fruit that had won him the Silver Cup at the Horticultural Society show, two weeks earlier.

Oswald took the basket of tomatoes with him and met the trainee at the marquee.

138

"Got your entry form, Roger?" Oswald placed the basket of fruit on the table and glanced at the other entries beside it. There was little competition but just to be sure he made a secret pass over the others and muttered a spell under his breath. The opposition began to wilt noticeably. Everything was going to Oswald's plan. Now there was little chance of Roger not winning as his fruit still looked as good as it had on the day he won the Silver Cup at the previous show.

John Buttadaeus followed the same routine he had for the first show. He arrived early, feigned an interest in everything and drifted to the fruit and vegetable tent. With Omni's warning still fresh in his memory he steeled himself to wait until the judging was over, so that he did not interfere with what must happen. He must not alter the past. That had cost him dearly in time and patience once already.

The judges left the beer tent reluctantly and started their rounds. Everyone else was ordered to leave the marquee so that they could deliberate in private.

"Beautiful beans; wonderful radishes. Pity about these tomatoes." The chairman voiced what they were all thinking. "Never seen such a poor lot. AND there's no entry from the Hall. Anybody know what Clay is up to, this year?"

They all shook their heads. Rumours had circulated of tomato thieves and there had been that unsolved pollution case when the river had flowed red, but nothing concrete had come of it all.

"This basket seems reasonable," one of the judges commented, lifting up Roger's entry. "But these others are all mouldy! Fancy putting tomatoes encrusted with penicillin into our show. It's a scandal!"

Police Sergeant Peele, still smarting from his failure to save the committee Oswald's fee, was in a parsimonious mood. He could see no reason to award the generous £100 prize for such a poor turnout.

"Can't we declare the competition void. Need we give anyone the prize money?"

The treasurer, who was worried about funding the annual Christmas blow-out, nodded vigorous agreement.

"There is a clear winner. I don't see how we can wriggle out of it," the vicar spoke up. He had been co-opted onto the panel as the allotments were mainly on glebe land.

The chairman, who was a keen student of tomatoes, picked up Roger's collection of fruit and eyed it thoughtfully.

"There's something funny about this little lot," he murmured. "I know one tomato looks very much like any other but I'd swear I've seen these before."

The secretary tipped the basket out onto the table so that they could get a better look. A Red card fell out with the fruit.

"Hello? What's this? Well I'll be damned! It's a place card awarded at the Horticultural Show, two weeks ago. It says, *'For best tomatoes in show'*. My trained policeman's nose smells something very fishy going on here."

"Does that mean they are the same fruit?" The vicar asked in a shocked voice.

"No, not exactly," the secretary murmured, "but I smell the hand of that bloody High Wizard in this." He could not see exactly how Oswald had influenced things in favour of his trainee but he dearly wanted to believe there had been foul play because he still had a chip on his shoulder about the weather fee.

"That settles it then. No contest."

The vicar shrugged his shoulders and stroked his nose. He thought the decision could be interpreted as grossly unfair to Roger.

"Maybe we could still declare Roger the winner, but withhold the prize money because there aren't enough good entries and we suspect these are the same fruit that won the other show."

140

"Well done, Vicar!" The chairman jumped at this face saving, money saving formula. The only problem he could see was what to tell the press.

A cub reporter from the Lincolnshire Free Monthly was following behind the judges, taking some photographs before the crowds descended on the marquee. His ears pricked up at this last remark. He sensed a juicy story. Flower and vegetable shows were uninteresting fodder, fit only for his newspaper's inside pages, that's why the reporting had been entrusted to him. A whiff of scandal would be manna from heaven and ensure him front-page coverage.

"Did you say these tomatoes won the show two weeks ago? How come they haven't rotted in that time."

"Perhaps they were kept in cold store?" The chairman suggested this, unconvincingly, for he knew that wouldn't work.

"No. I know all about cold stores. I did an article on banana importing, only last month. That won't wash,"

"Then you'd better ask the young man who entered them," the vicar suggested diplomatically.

Roger was in the beer tent, sipping a lemonade and keeping Oswald company. He had serious misgivings about the way his boss had fixed the tomato contest. This time he felt too uncomfortable to linger near the judging.

"Is there a young man called Roger, in there? The chap who entered the Tomato section of the show?"

The chemists' trainee heard the reporter call out his name and went out of the beer tent to see why he was needed.

"I'm Roger. Who wants me?"

"I'm the representative of the Lincolnshire News. Can you answer me a few questions about your entry?"

Roger coloured up crimson and looked most guilty. He had been dreading something like this. He nodded his head in dumb agreement.

"I understand you won the last show."

The lad nodded again.

"The judges say you entered the same tomatoes!" The reporter took the lad's breath away with that sudden accusation.

"Well yes...I suppose they are right, really."

The news hound smiled from ear to ear, his shock tactics had paid off. Here was an intriguing story for his readers.

"How did you manage to preserve ripe fruit in pristine condition for two whole weeks?" He asked triumphantly.

Oswald who was drinking his fill of free beer noticed his trainee had left the tent and not returned. He drifted to the entrance to see what was keeping him. Immediately he saw the reporter he realised things could be awkward. There was no way he could allow Roger to tell the press the High Wizard of the RUFS had performed some magic on the fruit. That would never do. He would be drummed out of the Wizards' guild, for breaking his vows of secrecy.

Oswald stepped in front of Roger and answered with the first thing that came into his mind "We used a new strain of Moneymaker we have been developing. We have done some genetic engineering on them."

The reporter's pen sped across his notebook.

"What exactly does this genetic engineering do to the tomatoes?"

"It probably makes them last forever." Oswald lied blatantly, the beer clouding his judgement and loosening his tongue.

"You mean, they will never rot? Never become inedible? That's fantastic."

Oswald, fearing he had already said too much, turned on his heels and marched back into the bar.

"Who was that gentleman?" The reporter asked Roger.

"He's my boss, Mr Gotobed, the pharmacist."

"Ah! So he's a trained scientist. He must know what he's talking about. Thank you, my boy."

142

He pressed a five-pound note into Roger's hand and dashed off to telephone his editor.

The confrontation outside the beer tent attracted a crowd of people. John Buttadaeus, standing on the periphery, listened delightedly to the conversation then moved smartly back to the marquee, intent on stealing the everlasting fruit. He now knew exactly where his quarry was. This time he had no intention of letting it slip through his fingers.

As soon as Oswald had digested the reporter's comments, he realised the judges must have tumbled to his plans to win the £100. Hurriedly he made his way to the exhibition tent and raced to the tomato stand. Roger trailed close behind him.

"Ah! I see we won, Roger." Oswald sighed with relief when he found the first place rosette pinned to the boy's basket.

"You were declared the best on the day but because of suspicions of foul play, you'll get no prize money." Greenfingers Clay gloated at them, from across the table. He had been patiently waiting, just to break that unwelcome news to his opponent.

"They can't do this!" Oswald shouted.

"We can and we have." Sgt Peele strode over, a triumphant grin on his face.

Oswald fumed and his chubby face turned deep purple. This was not just about prize fruit, this was revenge for having to pay his weather fee. He clenched his fists, shut his eyes and silently recited the antidote spell to the fine weather. There was a sudden clap of thunder, the skies opened and the crowds came rushing into the marquee to escape the downpour. The beer tent, the refreshment tent and any other shelter available was soon filled to capacity.

"Do your worst," the secretary shouted above the thunder. "We've sold a record number of tickets and now we'll sell a record amount of beer. It's too late for you to spoil things for us."

Oswald jumped up and down in temper.

"And I'm resigning from the RUFS. You can find another sucker to do your secretarial work."

Oswald lifted the basket of tomatoes from the table, intending to throw them over the secretary's head, but John Buttadaeus stepped in and restrained him with a firm hold on his forearm.

"Mr Gotobed, those prize tomatoes, wanted are they not?"

Oswald simmered down immediately. "Why? Do you want to buy them?"

"Gladly." John pulled a wad of ten pound notes from his pocket and handed them to the Druggist. "Here, my friend, a new wide hat buy yourself."

Oswald was delighted. There was at least two hundred pounds in that bundle of ten-pound notes. What did he care if this foreigner talked a load of rubbish and had no idea of the value of English money or of Moneymaker tomatoes. This windfall made up for his disappointment at the loss of the prize money. He grinned at Roger, who was standing by, silent and open mouthed in astonishment. The time traveller clutched his purchase close to his chest, smiled triumphantly, and strode out of the tent.

Chapter Twenty Six.

Saturday evening in Runford, settled into a normal routine, after the storms had passed, and the Allotment Holders annual fruit and Vegetable show was just a memory.

The young set, dressed in their best gear paraded in town between the chip shop and the Chinese takeaway, eyeing each other up and down before they made for the Youth Club disco. Paddy Murphy sat himself on his personal stool at the bar in the Dog in a Doublet and started his regular drinking marathon.

Big Frank Hogg settled down for a night alone at home, surrounding himself with beer cans and several packets of pork scratchings. He lined up his lucky rabbit's foot and a genuine Irish four leaf clover and sat in front of the television. It was lottery draw night.

Frank had misgivings about this lottery business. Everything else he had done with the time machine had gone wrong. Even the oil painting he had brought back for Theo Willis, appeared to have been stolen; not that it was worth much. He really couldn't understand the antique dealer's intense disappointment at the loss of something of so little value. Then there was his motorbike, that had been miraculously saved only to be damaged in exactly the same place as before. Frank was superstitious, believing, like many of his fenland neighbours, that troubles came in threes; causing him even more mixed feelings about the lottery draw.

The build up and hype to the choosing of the numbered lottery balls was designed to heighten the tension in every British household. Frank didn't usually bother with it. He checked his numbers in the newspaper later in the week, much preferring to go on the beer on a Saturday night. But this week was different. This week he had supernatural help in choosing his numbers and he felt his future happiness with Freda depended on the outcome.

The lottery show ran true to form. Two flunkies in dark suits with white cotton gloves loaded the balls into the chosen machine. A blonde bimbo announced the arrival of the Minister for Sport, who was to press the starter button for that particular run of the national gamble. Mystic Felicity, the resident fortune teller, was wheeled onto the set, complete with crystal ball and Tarot cards.

"I see a Hell's Angel with a four leaf clover in his hand, winning a big jackpot this week."

Frank grabbed his lucky clover and put his beer glass down.

"I also see a dear white haired old grandmother and some shop girls..." They wheeled her off before she could finish; they were running behind schedule.

The first numbered ball out of the spin drier, matched one of Frank's selection. He nodded appreciatively. The second and third numbers also matched his card. He held his breath, stopped chewing his pork scratchings in mid crunch and rechecked his numbers.

"I'm already ten pound better off!" He whooped, spattering the television screen with a fine layer of damp scratchings.

The next number out of the machine matched Frank's just as the previous three had. The big man whimpered. The tension was unbelievable.

Ball five fell according to plan. Frank was definitely in the big money.

He hid his face behind a cushion and squinted at the screen between his fingers, willing the bonus ball to match his last number but not daring to look properly. Visions of taking Freda on the holiday of a lifetime, chrome plating his entire motorbike, and getting his clock lathe out of pawn, floated before him.

The bonus ball was called. It matched Frank's final number!

"I'm rich! I'm a bloody millionaire!" Frank threw his packet of pork bits in the air and danced around the room, carelessly trampling the greasy titbits into the carpet. Once he had calmed down, he telephoned the women's refuge, asking to speak to his wife. Gabby came to the phone.

"You again! Don't you ever give up?"

"Tell Freda I've won the lottery. Tell her me numbers have come up."

"If I have my way, your number will definitely come up!"

"Tell her me balls have fallen right."

"All you men ever think about is sex and getting your rocks off!" Gabby slammed down the receiver.

In other parts of Runford the newsagent's staff were celebrating similarly. Their manager had persuaded them all to wager a pound on the winning numbers.

The grey haired old lady, who had sold Frank the oil painting for fifty pounds, was oblivious to her windfall. She was enjoying herself at the over eighties Bingo.

Frank opened all his remaining cans of beer, poured them into a cut glass flower vase and guzzled the lot. He switched off his Television and ignored all the later programs.

During the late news, the TV announcer beamed at camera one. "There are twelve winners who share in tonight's jackpot of twelve million pounds. Strangely, they all seem to live in the same town in south Lincolnshire."

Security experts at Lottery headquarters were feverishly checking their computers, suspecting foul play. A cluster of twelve individual winners in one small town, was unheard of. It had never happened before.

Chapter Twenty Seven.

Lydia Postlethwaite always tidied the guest rooms on a Saturday. It was changeover day, the day her guests usually left, and she liked to prepare the rooms for any newcomers. She vacuumed and dusted John Buttadaeus' room, pleasantly surprised at the tidiness of it. There were no crumbs or greasy chip papers, nothing in the waste bin and the bed looked as if it hadn't been slept in. He was the kind of lodger she appreciated for he was no trouble and exceedingly cheap to feed, as he ate nothing. She opened the wardrobe to check in there and was dazzled by his metallic suit.

What would a normal man want with a silver lame jacket and trousers, she asked herself? He didn't look the kind of man to wear way-out dress like that. He couldn't be a closet transvestite, could he? The shiny clothes intrigued her so much, she took them down and fingered the material.

Lydia was a lady of ample proportions; the constant availability of bar snacks and alcohol were her undoing. She consoled herself with the thought that men liked a barmaid with something to spill onto the counter, other than the beer.

The temptation to try on the Silver outfit proved too much for her. Lydia slipped into the jacket. It fitted her like a glove. It hung on her as if it was made for her. This surprised her somewhat, as her lodger was a tall slim gentleman. Similarly the slim trousers seemed to adjust to her measurements and even though her waistline was at least half as big again as John's, the slacks expanded to fit her comfortably.

"I could just do with a suit that fits any size and does it elegantly," she muttered. "I wonder who his tailor is?" She was just removing the jacket to search for the label when her lodger arrived home. "Oh! Do excuse me, Mr Buttadaeus. I was cleaning up your room and I just fell in love with this silver lame number. Is it a present for your wife? Do tell me where you bought it."

John was taken aback at this intrusion into his privacy. His first thought was to put down his carrier bag of tomatoes and grab Lydia by the neck, putting her into a trance, but he was in a jubilant mood; he had at last obtained the tomatoes he had come for.

"Where I saw it for sale I cannot exactly remember. When I do remember, I'll let you know."

Lydia detected some slight annoyance in his voice and hurriedly put the suit back on its hanger and left him in peace.

"Omni, it's good that we have at last found the everlasting fruit, but the natives are getting too inquisitive. I have stayed here too long already." He didn't get a reply from his minute computer for he hadn't asked a question. The time traveller carefully took Roger's winning basket of Moneymaker from his plastic carrier bag and stood it in pride of place on the bedside cabinet.

"Tonight after dark, we will replace these levers on our time machine and go back to our own century." He took the two brass rods from his pocket and held them up to show the black box.

Omni kept its own counsel. It had already scanned the winning tomatoes and found them to be nothing out of the ordinary.

Oswald Gotobed, High Wizard of the RUFS had had a mixed day. He had made two hundred pounds selling Roger's tomatoes, but he had also fallen out with the Union secretary, who had resigned. Filling the vacant post would not be easy and making an enemy of a local police sergeant was never wise.

"Some you win, and some you lose," he said philosophically. "Now I'd better remove that preservation spell from those tomatoes or they'll finish up in the national papers and I'll be forced to explain how I did it." The Wizard recited the Latin antidote and projected it onto the ether.

John Buttadaeus rested, hovering inches above the bed, his eyes closed, his mind still. He would need all his energies to work on the genetic makeup of the fruit, as soon as he returned to his laboratory in the 26th century. Omni was perched on the bedside cabinet watching and waiting.

At ten o'clock, as it got dark, the old man roused himself from his rest and changed into his aluminium suit. A faint whiff of cheap perfume wafted from the jacket as he took it from the hanger.

"It's high time we left. I think that female is laying scent to attract me," he grumbled to Omni.

The black box stirred its olfactory circuits and detected other molecules in the air. There was a definite hint of mustiness. It focused on the basket beside it on the cabinet.

"The tomatoes. They seem to be ageing rapidly, master!"

John spun around in dismay, caught his foot in his trouser leg, as he was still putting them on, and fell on the bedroom floor.

"What do you mean alarming me like that? I could have broken something!"

Omni cleared its artificial throat nervously and answered in a hurt tone.

150

"I only thought you would want to know that your tomatoes are mouldy."

John leapt to the cabinet, grabbed the basket in his hand and took it to the centre of the room, where the light was brighter. He grasped one of the wrinkled fruit in his hand and squeezed it to check the firmness. Rotting pulp ran between his fingers, dark juice and seeds dripped down his silver sleeve. The strong smell of decay filled the room.

"Damn! Damn!" He shouted again. "That tubby scoutmaster had duped me! I will get even with the little bastard. We must find him and force him to tell us the secret of eternal life."

On Sunday morning Malcolm always attended early communion at the parish church. He was surprised to be joined on his walk by the elderly stranger he had first met at the churchyard.

"Going to the early service?" The Chemist beamed at his companion. "If you ask the vicar afterwards I'm sure he'll know if any of your ancestors are buried in the churchyard."

As they passed by the RUFS' building in the High Street, John Buttadaeus put his hand on Malcolm's shoulder in a seemingly friendly gesture. But he pushed his long fingers into the nerve plexus near the Chemist's neck and instantly paralysed him.

"Follow me." John entered the Union library, closely followed by Malcolm Gotobed, who was looking straight ahead like someone sleepwalking. They climbed the stairs to the attic where John tried to question the Chemist about the everlasting tomatoes.

"The real everlasting fruit, what have you done with it?"

"I don't know what you mean," Malcolm intoned.

"Silly beggars, do not with me play." John lost his temper. "Regret it you will, if you help me not."

151

He took Omni from his pocket and placed it in front of Malcolm on the attic floor, where it could analyse his speech patterns and act as a lie detector.

"The only tomatoes I know about are the one's Roger entered for the vegetable show."

Omni buzzed its agreement.

"They are those!" John yelled.

"I think my twin brother put a spell on them to make them last longer," Malcolm answered in a flat tone.

"Rubbish! You the High Wizard are. I myself heard your lecture. You the tomatoes bewitched. If anybody did."

"No."

Omni buzzed his agreement once more but that was not what its master wanted to hear.

The time traveller was about to try other more physical means of persuasion on his unfortunate hostage when he heard the front door slam shut. Someone was in the library below him.

"Get on that leather seat," he hissed in his victim's ear.

Malcolm sat down on the clock frame as composed as if he was accompanying his wife, playing hymns on the harmonium in his own front room.

Below, in the library, Oswald was looking for his notes on the time machine. He remembered shutting them in one of the grimoires when Theo had disturbed his researches. Now he wished to check them against the frame of the turret clock, to try and work out their functions. After several minutes of fruitless searching, the Wizard ran out of patience and started to climb the spiral staircase to the attic room.

John Buttadaeus panicked and jumped aboard his time machine. In his hurry, he completely forgot to pick up his computerised black box.

Oswald heard the machine start up as he reached the top step. He looked up in amazement, just in time to see his brother and the silver clad foreigner vanish into thin air.

The turret clock and its two passengers dissolved before the Wizard's eyes.

"Come back with my brother," he yelled at the top of his voice.

The clock vanished. The attic fell silent. The Wizard was alone. They had gone completely.

Chapter Twenty Eight.

There was a queue of impatient customers at the door of the Runford newsagents.

"We never got our Sun, this morning. Me old man wont go to the courtroom without his paper," The magistrate's wife shouted through the letterbox of the closed shop.

"I always start the week with Monday's Times crossword. My wife devours the fashion pages," the dustcart driver confided to another distraught customer in the queue.

No one had turned up for work at the newsagents. Rumours were rife. Some idiot even suggested the staff syndicate had won the lottery and they were all now millionaires. A police car drove onto the High Street and screeched to a halt in front of the shop.

"You'll have to do without your Beano today, officer," the dustman quipped.

"Move along there please. Break up this gathering. The shop will not be opening today. The staff are all at the police station helping us with our enquiries."

That really set the tongues wagging. Some suggested they had been selling pornographic magazines, others thought they had raided the till.

Frank Hogg had been awakened by the police, banging on his door at five o'clock that morning. He heard their far off voices through the alcoholic haze of his celebrations.

"Come on Frank, we know you're in there."

Frank stumbled down the stairs, bleary eyed and dry mouthed and opened the door to his caller.

"Just routine." The officer smiled; he was a motorcyclist himself and he knew the Hell's Angel for the gentle man he really was. "It's about your lottery win. I just need to confirm at what time you filled in your winning card."

Frank gave him the information, producing his till receipt to prove it. The officer compared that with the time given by the lottery computer.

"Did you tell anybody else your numbers, Frank?"

"Yes, I sure did; to a little old lady with grey hair. She didn't seem to know what numbers to use." The policeman nodded and checked his records again. There was another winning line two minutes after Frank's.

"I've sent off me ticket by registered post. Is everything alright?"

"Everything's fine, Frank. You're a lucky devil by the sounds of it."

"Why this query then?"

"The Lottery organisers think there's been some foul play. The entire staff of the newsagents used the same numbers as you. Only they did it half an hour after you and the old lady, according to the computer read out. The lottery people are loath to pay out as they think it's some clever fraud. But that won't effect you, will it."

"I hope not." Frank breathed a sigh of relief at this news. Perhaps he had been hasty, thinking things were going wrong in threes.

The grey haired old lady, who's favourite grandson just happened to be a detective at the Runford police station, was not included in the investigation. Elderly females always seem to throw a six, as far as the game of Cops and Robbers is concerned. Perhaps if Bonnie and Clyde had lived into old age things would have been different for Bonnie

The Lottery organisers decided not to pay out to the newsagents staff.

155

They made up some excuse that staff were excluded from taking part in the game, but that was the first anybody had heard of that rule. The ten million pounds was put on ice until the courts could decide the matter. A slick American lawyer, specialising in victimisation cases, flew over on Concorde and offered to take up the staff's case with the court, for a fee of 50% of their winnings and all TV rights on the Justice Channel. It was all getting terribly messy.

Frank Hogg never left the house the remainder of that week. He wanted to be at home when the postman delivered his cheque. There was to be no publicity; he had specified as much on his application, because he wanted to surprise Freda with his new-found wealth.

"If she wont leave the refuge, I'll buy it for her and move in there with her and her friends," he vowed naively.

That afternoon the little old lady came to see him. She arrived by taxi, flung her arms around his neck and kissed him.

"You are my lucky mascot. First you bought that worthless old painting from me, then you gave me the winning lottery numbers. You must be a real angel from heaven, not a Hell's Angel like my neighbours called you."

Frank blushed, rinsed out two mugs and invited her in for tea and some pork scratchings.

Chapter Twenty Nine

Frank Hogg was waiting at the gate, the morning his lottery cheque was delivered. He took the official looking envelope in shaking hands and rushed back into the house.

"Morning Frank. You're in a hell of a hurry!" The postman shouted after him. As soon as nine o'clock struck Frank fired up the Harley and drove into town to open an account with the Runford Building Society. The cheque for a Million Pounds nestled safely in his pocket, next to his heart. At last he knew he had something that would bring Freda back to him.

"Come into my private office." The branch manager invited the Hell's Angel into his inner sanctum, once he had confirmed the number of noughts on the Lottery cheque.

"Have a cigar. Congratulations, old man."

"I don't smoke, but I'll have a beer with you."

The office junior was dispatched urgently to the off-licence for a four pack.

"Now, Mr Hogg, may I call you Frank? What type of account did you have in mind?" The manager spread a fan of multicoloured leaflets on the desktop, with the dexterity of a card sharp. "We have a ninety-day, easy access, account which pays a whole one percent interest, and an investment account which gives you a further generous half percent on top of that. Of course, we will need the usual six months notice of withdrawal, on that account. There are TESSAS and PEPS and the staff benevolent fund. My wife runs a charity..." He got no further.

"I want to put the cheque in today and withdraw it all in cash tomorrow." Frank interrupted.

The manager coughed violently. Either the beer had gone down wrong way or something Frank had said was sticking in his throat.

"Take it all out! All the lot? What's the use of putting it into savings just to take it all out again?"

"I need it in cash. All the lot, in new fifty-pound notes. I want to hold it in my hands and let my wife run her fingers through it."

"There's always a delay while the cheque clears, you understand?"

"I'll wait 'til the weekend. If I can't have it by then I'll go somewhere else."

The manager closed his eyes to cut out the vision of his bonus flying out of the window. He had already decided where he was going to go on an exotic holiday.

"We will try. Just hang on a minute while I ring head office." He left Frank with a further can of beer and went into the main office to telephone the lottery people to confirm the genuiness of the cheque. If they said yes, he knew he couldn't lose. This business of needing to see the money in bank notes was typical of the local country yokels; they wouldn't believe anything until they actually saw it with their own eyes and touched it with their grubby fingers.

158

Give the idiot a day or two to play with his winnings like monopoly money and he'd be back with the vast majority of it to invest.

"We can do it, Mr Hogg, as a special dispensation for a valued customer. We wouldn't do it for less than a Mill... I mean we would only do it for a trusted customer like yourself."

Frank left the office satisfied with his morning's work. His brand new passbook nestled warmly inside his jacket pocket. He hummed contentedly to himself as he revved up the Harley and thought of the surprise Freda would get.

Chapter Thirty

Oswald Gotobed raced down the spiral staircase from the attic.   He had arrived just too late to catch John Buttadaeus, Malcolm and the time machine.   There was no time to waste. He must search the Spell Books for some way to follow his brother into the space time continuum or to bring the turret clock back to the present.

The High Wizard piled the books on the table and feverishly went through them. He needed to master advanced Time Magic as quickly as possible. Heaven knows what awful fate awaited his twin brother if he failed to sort out his disappearance.

As he thumbed through the books he thought over the events of that day. That foreigner must be some kind of Wizard or at least an advanced adept at Time Travelling.   Malcolm could be lost in any place and at any time; a time/space traveller had the whole universe and the entire calendar at his disposal. He adjusted his reading glasses and shifted his speed reading into top gear. Unfortunately he was disturbed; there was a loud knocking on the street door below.

"Who the devil's that interrupting me when I'm busy?" Oswald grumbled, wondering whether he could ignore the caller.

The hammering grew louder. The door reverberated with the impact. Whoever was out there, meant business.

160

"It's the police. We know you're there Oswald Gotobed. Come down and let us in." Sergeant Peele's voice bellowed from below.

Oswald slammed his book shut and reluctantly went down to open the front door. "What the hell's this noise? I hope..." He got no further.

"Grab him constable. Bring him down to the police station," Peele shouted.

Before Oswald could draw another breath to make an excuse or cast a spell, he was clapped into handcuffs and bundled into the waiting squad car. At the police station he was manhandled into the interrogation room and forced to sit under a bright light.

"Tell us where you got all the ten pound notes you've been spending?"

Oswald relaxed. Now he knew there had been some mistake. Spending ten-pound notes was hardly a criminal offence.

"Stop messing about, Peele. Loosen my hands."

"Not damn likely. I saw what happened to that glass of beer when you made your magic passes over it."

"Well at least let me phone the shop to tell Roger to get a locum pharmacist in for the day."

"We questioned Roger earlier. He already knows what's happening. Now what about these ten pound notes?"

"The only ten pound notes I have are the one's I was given at the Allotment Holders' Show."

"In your change from the bar? What did you pay with, fifty-pound notes? Anyway we both know that's a lie, you were on a free pass. Gotcha!" Peele said triumphantly."

"No. Some old chap gave me £200 for the basket of tomatoes that won the first prize."

"Oh yes! A likely story! And my officer here, painted Constable's Haywain I suppose? £200 for a basket of tomatoes?

I ask you. I expected a High Wizard to conjure up a better excuse than that. Can't you do any better?"

"Go and ask the man. He's lodging at the Dog..." Oswald faltered, he didn't actually know where the foreigner had gone.

"What do you know about similar ten pound notes planted on innocent fishermen?"

Oswald shook his head in disbelief. If he had some spare money, fishermen would be the last people to get a hand out. His opinion of those sportsmen was extremely low. One of his favourite remarks was, 'If you are walking by the river and you catch sight of a cane with a worm dangling at each end, that's a fisherman.'

"Your trainee had five of these same notes, given to him by you at the vegetable show. He's admitted as much."

"I've told you once. An old gentleman handed them to me in payment for the tomatoes. That was Roger's cut."

"Yes, sir, we know all about it. Lord Lucan won the cucumber class and Shurgar was giving donkey rides to the children behind the beer tent! It's no good trying to implicate an innocent youth. Young Roger wouldn't stoop to such crime." Peele stalked up and down the room, slapping his truncheon threateningly against the palm of his hand. He turned and glowered at his prisoner.

"We've check with the banks. There was a similar, coffee stained bank note handed in with your shop takings last week. How do you account for that?" The sergeant continued pacing up and down the room, like a caged tiger with time on its paws.

"Lydia Postlethwaite tried to bank several more of those bank notes. And you drink at her place most nights. What about that?"

"I'm not the only person who drinks at that pub."

"Perhaps not, but it's too much of a coincidence. These notes keep following you around." Sgt Peele smiled secretly in the shadows. The policeman was enjoying himself; he had a score to settle with the High Wizard.

162

"Anyway, what's wrong with owning ten pound notes? I bet you've got one or two in your pocket."

"Yes, but mine aren't forgeries!" The sergeant halted in front of the Druggist, pushed the prisoner's head back with the tip of his truncheon and glared into his upturned face.

Oswald bit his lip. Now he began to understand. That old man had paid him with forged notes. No wonder he paid over the odds for a basket of fruit. He must have passed several more at the pub and probably spent one at the pharmacy. But why had he kidnapped Malcolm and vanished into thin air with him? That bloody foreigner had a lot to answer for.

Chapter Thirty One

The bell of Runford church clock struck eleven o'clock. The sounds reverberated through the damp night air, even reaching into the police cells. Oswald sat on the bare mattress on the bed in his prison, his knees drawn up under his chin, his handcuffed wrists resting on the top of them.

"What a time to try and get even with me. Peele is only helping the real culprit make his getaway." The Wizard was tired and hungry after the prolonged questioning and even though the police had fetched fish and chips over to his cell he hadn't the heart to eat them, not with his brother in danger. He had tried telling the sergeant that someone had kidnapped his twin but Peele only laughed and told him to try another excuse. Oswald couldn't really blame the policeman for not believing his story; it was difficult for him to believe it himself.

Long after pub closing time, when there was a lull at the police station, Oswald decided it was time to make his move. As High Wizard he had enough tricks up his sleeve to give the local coppers a run for their money. He waited until all was quiet, slipped off his shoes, a task made easier by the lack of laces, and propped them up against the window bars with the soles uppermost. The Wizard recited the invisibility spell. Slowly he vanished into thin air. He was still handcuffed and had difficulty holding up his invisible trousers because they had confiscated his belt, but he managed to stand behind the cell door and yell for help.

The night duty constable heard the racket and came to investigate. He pushed aside the string of garlic bulbs that Peele had hung on the door, and slid back the observation hatch to peer in at the prisoner. Oswald was nowhere to be seen!

"Eh up! He's escaped! The sergeant said there was a slippery customer in this cell but he didn't tell me it was bloody Houdini!" The constable threw open the cell door and stepped inside. The first thing he noticed was Oswald's shoes, resting soles uppermost, on the window ledge. He rushed over to the window.

"He's jumped through the bars, leaving his shoes behind him!"

The constable had hardly uttered these words when the cell door swung shut behind him, with a resounding clang. The key, which he had stupidly left in the door, grated as invisible fingers locked the policeman inside.

It took five more minutes for Oswald to locate the handcuff key among the collection on the ring and to unlock his bracelets. Then he tiptoed along the row of cells, unlocking every other door so that the criminals and the drunks, sleeping off their revels, could escape. Rounding up that lot would keep the local police busy for the rest of the night. The invisible Wizard slunk out of the police station and made for the Union building, treading gingerly across the hard pavements in his bare feet.

Once he was safely locked in the RUFS library, the Wizard opened the emergency supply of candles and climbed the spiral stairs to check if the turret clock had returned. One glance from the top of the iron staircase was enough to confirm his worst fears. The clock, the foreigner and his twin brother were still not there. In the shadows he did not notice the small back box dropped there by John Buttadaeus.

Oswald collected the Magic books again. He read them by a flickering candle flame, sitting under the table to avoid detection. No stray light alerted passersby to his presence.

He was confident the police would be too occupied to miss him until the morning, but even if they did discover his escape they would hardly expect him to come straight back to the place where he was arrested. He felt he had a breathing space until daylight returned. But would it provide enough time for him to help Malcolm?

"If only I knew where they'd gone? Could it be the past or maybe they went into the future? If I knew which way, I would know where to look in the spelling books." Oswald talked to himself for company and for reassurance. He flicked over page after page of archaic writing, reading the Latin script until his eyes ached in the poor light. By three o'clock in the morning he had dozed off under the library table. The candle had burned down and spluttered out leaving a faint trail of smoke, rising in the cool air.

"Beep, beep, beep, beep!" Oswald woke up with a start and in his confusion assumed the candle smoke had set off a smoke alarm.

"Rubbish! We haven't fitted smoke alarms in the library."

The faint sound that had disturbed his sleep, could still be heard and it seemed to be coming from the attic above him. He crept up the spiral staircase, noiseless on his bare feet, and peered over the top step into the pitch darkness. Disappointingly, there was no sign of the time machine, but from the far corner, he could still hear the beeping sound. It grew louder as he crawled towards it.

Oswald struck a match, fearful of what he might find. The sounds seemed to come from near his feet. His first thought was of rats in the attic. Could it be a musical rodent? It was a strange sound. Maybe it came from one of those computer mice Roger often talked about; it was certainly an electronic note. At first there seemed nothing to see when he lit up that corner of the attic floor. The match had almost burned down to his fingers before he noticed a small black matchbox, in the shadows.

166

"Just an empty matchbox!"

Omni beeped again. This time a faint red light flickered on. Oswald picked up the small box in the pitch dark and crept back to the top of the iron steps, feeling his way hand over hand.

Back under the table with a new candle alight in the holder, the Wizard examined his find. There was no longer an electronic note issuing from the thing, nor was there a red warning light. All was silent and black. He turned it over in his sweaty hand and tried pushing the slide open to see if there were any matches inside, for he was getting low in his own supply. But he couldn't find a way to open it.

"Damn funny matchbox! Black is a stupid colour for an object one would need to find when the lights go off!"

Omni held its breath. It had activated its alarm to tell its master that it had been left behind, before it had detected the invisible presence in the library. For once in its career the omniscient miniature computer had met something new. It only took a minute for the box to switch to its infra red detection range instead of the visible spectrum, then it became aware of the invisible Wizard.

Other strange things seemed to be happening to the electronic know-all. At first Omni suspected a malfunction in its circuits for the human that held it, was identical in appearance to the man its master had taken away on the time machine. Could they be twins? To find the answer it proceeded to analyse the DNA of its finder, from the traces of sweat left on its sides. It tried to detect the small genetic differences that even identical twins must display. It was then, the black box got an even bigger shock.

Chapter Thirty Two.

The Building Society did Frank Hogg proud. They waived the usual time for a cheque to clear, once they were certain the lottery had enough funds to honour the winnings. At eight o'clock that morning the Security Core armoured van rolled up to the big man's front door to deliver one million pounds in new fifty -pound notes.

"Sign here for twenty thousand bank notes, please mate."

Frank stared boggle eyed, struck dumb, and paralysed by the enormity of it all. He picked up one of the bundles and rifled through it like a pack of cards.

"I hope you don't want to check every bundle, mate. We ain't got all day."

Frank recovered his senses and signed the receipt. The guards carried all the bundles of currency into his workshop and piled them on his workbench.

The big man slowly washed and shaved, every few minutes sneaking back to his workbench to look at his windfall.

"Freda won't believe her eyes. She won't believe it..." he kept repeating to himself in the shaving mirror. After breakfast Frank pulled one of the fifty-pound notes from the top bundle and covered over the remainder with an old tartan blanket for security. He even locked the door as he left the house, something he rarely bothered to do, as there was usually nothing of value in the place. Then he went to town.

The newsagent was open but there was no one there that he recognised, and the new staff couldn't find anything. He guessed they must be relief staff, standing in for the disputed lottery winners.

"Show me the largest box of chocolates you have in the shop and I'll want a greeting card to go with it."

"There's a huge Creamtray selection box under the stairs," one girl whispered to the other. "It was left over from Valentine's day, last year."

"Surely that one will be stale by now," the first assistant whispered back.

Frank leaned over the counter and joined in their private conversation. He said in a loud stage whisper. "That doesn't matter. No one's going to eat them."

The shop girls giggled and fetched the giant box of chocolates. They checked his fifty-pound note, holding it up to the light and pushing it under the new ultra violet forgery detector that head office had supplied; they had been warned by the police to keep an eye out for dud notes.

Frank took the huge box with the crimson heart emblazoned across it and strapped it securely to his motorbike seat. He drove slowly home, avoiding all the bumps in the road and any reversing tractors.

The chocolates in their frilly brown paper cases, looked oddly lost in the wheelie bin when Frank tipped the box contents away. Neither he nor Freda ate sweets. He removed the padding from the box and refilled it with the bundles of new fifty-pound notes, laid in neat rows to replace the confectionery. Where there had been old, stale soft-centres, now there was new, crisp, bank notes. It was a regular box of delights. Surely, it would be the way to any woman's heart?

"I'll surprise Freda. She'll come running back to me when she knows I'm a millionaire." The Hell's Angel resealed the box with sticky tape, tied a large red ribbon around it for added safety and tucked the greeting card under the knot.

His surprise package completed, he telephoned his motorcycling mates to tell them that he would need an escort to accompany him to the women's refuge. He did not mention money but let them believe he had bought the biggest box of chocolates in Runford and wanted to deliver it with due ceremony. Most of his fellow Angels agreed to turn out and ride with him; the one's with jobs needed little excuse to skip work for the day and ride their bikes.

At ten o'clock sharp they assembled at Frank Hogg's cottage. The air in the lane was blue with exhaust fumes. The revving of their throttles drowned out any other sounds. Frank proudly took his place at the head of the procession. The chocolate box was fixed securely to his broad back with elastic luggage straps.

"Ain't it romantic, Julie? Just like that bloke who jumps from aeroplanes, skis down mountainsides and sneaks into your bedroom. And all because the lady fancies Creamtray chocolates. I'd prefer he stopped for a bit of the other, but there's no accounting for her taste! Why don't some lovely fella treat me like that?" Samantha settled her ample leather clad rear onto her creaking motorbike saddle and wiped a sentimental tear from under her visor.

The phalanx of roaring motorcycles headed for the town. News of the gathering spread quickly and crowds poured out of homes, schools and offices along the route, to wave them on. The police soon got wind of the procession and joined in as motorcycle escorts. Frank Hogg smiled contentedly to himself as he headed the biker throng. He felt like King Arthur leading his band of trusty followers. His pony tail trailed out behind his helmet, like the plume on a knight's jousting helm. The oblong chocolate box was slung over his back like a shield. The South Lincolnshire Chapter of Hell's Angels banner fluttered from a brush pole tied to his motorbike forks. He cut a dashing figure, reminding many of the onlookers of the jousting knights they'd seen on the TV.

170

At the edge of town, they were joined by a bigger, official escort. A dozen police motorcyclists with sirens blaring and blue lights flashing cleared their way. Nothing had been seen like it in Runford since Garry Glitter had opened the local canning factory.

The phalanx of riders halted at the railway crossing while a goods train chugged by. The police checked with the signal box to make sure no more trains were due for half an hour, then waved the riders through.

The inmates of the Women's Refuge had come out to see what the commotion was about, but when they spotted all the motorcyclists they retreated indoors and bolted the doors. Quite a few of the women were married to Hell's Angels; the others were fearful of the bikers' reputations.

Gabby took charge of the group, her subversive experience at Greenham Common stood her in good stead. She made them duck under the windows and watch from behind the curtains. She fancied herself as an urban guerrilla. The women watched as the motorcyclists halted at the gate. None of the riders went inside the grounds, for news had spread of Frank's roasting with the weed gun. Frank propped his Harley-Davidson at the kerbside, and took his helmet off, holding it under his arm like a knight errant approaching his lady. Fearlessly he stalked into the empty yard and placed the chocolate box on the path, several paces from the locked front door.

"That's for you Freda," he shouted to the empty windows. Then he retreated with dignity, walking backwards to his yellow motorbike. The crowd of motorcyclists clapped madly and cheered like supporters at a football match.

Frank sat in the gateway on his iron stead, waiting for something to happen. The riders switched off their engines and silence fell outside the refuge. It was like a stand-off in an armed siege. Each side eyeing the other warily. Each side weighing up the opposition.

Gabby took her urban guerrilla role very seriously and ordered her helpers to collect an item from the garden shed at the rear of the building. Out of sight of the road they crept stealthily across the back lawn like freedom fighters and located the large tin of weed killer their leader had demanded.

"Sugar," Gabby whispered.

"No need to swear," the vicar's wife protested. She had joined the group when she had stumbled across twenty more pairs of mixed knickers in her husband's car boot.

"Castor sugar, preferably; it mixes better."

Gabby mixed the weed killer and the sugar and put them in an empty, catering-size cocoa tin. She inserted a string fuse and explained her plan to the others.

"They can't buy our favours with a box of chocolates."

"Why not?" One of the weaker sisters asked.

"It's immoral, degrading and fattening for a start."

"Lets show them we can't be bought... We're like a tree that's standing by the water. We shall not be moved." The vicar's wife took up the refrain and the protest; she'd always fancied herself in the role of church martyr. Freda kept unusually quiet.

As the Hell's Angels kept their silent vigil outside the gates the front door of the hostel swung open. Everyone leaned forward, expecting a deputation to accept the gift on Freda's behalf but the doorway remained empty. No one came forward.

After several tense minutes two masked women rolled the large cocoa tin across the yard and planted it next to the chocolate box.

Silence reigned once again as the door closed behind the two anonymous women. All seemed to be exactly as before. No one in the crowd outside, noticed the wisp of smoke snaking along the fuse towards the cocoa drum.

The explosion took all the leather-clad spectators by surprise. It blew the chocolate box up into the sky and catapulted Frank off his legs.

172

A huge plume of flame and smoke mushroomed above Runford like a gigantic Guy Fawkes rocket. The paper bank-notes ignited instantly, lending a golden glow to the morning sky. The money flared momentarily, in an expensive blaze of glory then showered down in a gnat rain of curly white ash, covering the entire town in a fine grey layer. It was the shortest million pound firework display in the county's history.

Inside the refuge, the women were jubilant at their success. Those men could stuff their chocolates. Gabby flung her arms around Freda and kissed her passionately. Freda pushed her away and rubbed off the taste of her lipstick, with the back of her hand.

Outside, Frank was the first to move. He picked himself up and dusted himself down, thankful for his protective leathers. The loss of the money didn't bother him. Easy come, easy go was his philosophy. But he was devastated that Freda had made no effort to come out to see him. He turned to the nearest Hell's Angel swore loudly and started up his motor bike. The rest of the Chapter had not recovered from the shock of the explosion when Frank accelerated off from the kerbside, heading into town. The big man left his followers standing open-mouthed in amazement.

"I'll ride that damn time machine again, if it's the last thing I do. I'll make replacement brass levers for the thing and go back to the day that Gabriella first knocked on our door. I'll not let her into the house. She can take her bloody bake bean recipes and her bolshi ideas and push off somewhere else"

Chapter Thirty Three

Oswald hid himself in the RUFS' library, to keep out of the way of the police. He was a wanted man since his escape from the cells. In normal circumstances he would have worked to clear his name but now the only thing on his mind was fear for his brother's safety. The Wizard spent all his time studying the Union's collection of Magic books, searching for a time spell to bring back his twin. His own safety was last on his list.

Oswald reversed the invisibility spell, once he felt he was secure, and padded about the library carpet in his bare feet. This relieved him of the need to maintain the vanishing spell and allowed him to concentrate unhindered on his research. Each time he found a new time spell, any sort of time spell, he made a note on a sheet of scrap paper. When the sheaf of jottings grew large and untidy, Oswald looked around for something to anchor them down. He picked up the black matchbox; it was the nearest thing to hand, and placed it on top of his notes to act as a paperweight.

"Nothing! Not one single bloody spell to bring back a lost time machine! Plenty of time magic, but none to do with time machines. The damn things weren't invented when these old books were written. Of course, it would help if I knew which direction the turret clock had travelled. Is it in the future or the past? I haven't a clue which way it went. Why couldn't it have a sign on it like the number twenty seven bus to Deeping Fen?"

The Wizard immersed himself deeper in his work. He kidded himself he was doing something useful, but he knew he was really wasting his time, unless the old man chose to return of his own free will. The morning passed; Oswald climbed up and down the library steps, back and forth to the table and his jottings. It was activity for the sake of it, like an ant in a stirred up nest. He would do anything to stay busy and take his mind off Malcolm.

"What if they never come back? What if that old man murders Malcolm or leaves him stranded in some past century? I know my brother would cope with life in another time. Malcolm's the sort to adapt. But then, I'd never see him again! I've never told him this to his face. He's not such a bad old stick. I'm very fond of him really."

Omni stood on the reams of paper, where he had been placed as a paper weight and listened to the monologue with only half an electronic ear for it had problems of equal importance on its own mind circuits.

The Wizard slammed the final volume shut and rubbed his tired eyes. Being awake most of the night, reading the archaic, hand written Latin script by candlelight was beginning to tell on him.

"If only I knew why that bloody foreigner made off with Malcolm in the first place. If only there was some way to contact the blighter. A box number, a forwarding address, a mobile telephone: even one of those new fangled E-mail or fax numbers would help."

Omni cleared its mechanical throat and coughed in a high pitched, childlike way. It had decided to make its presence known.

"What the devil's that?" Oswald stopped his reading and looked around the room for the source of the noise. "Who's there?"

"It's me. The black box you are using as a paperweight."

"What are you, some sort of Shapeshifter or faerie? Come out of hiding and let me see you properly." Oswald ordered the unseen presence.

"I'm here on top of your notes. I'm the little black matchbox you picked up in the attic."

The Wizard recoiled from the desk, eyeing the talking box as suspiciously as he would a bomb.

"Matchboxes don't talk," he said emphatically. "Well, not unless I choose to put a spell on them, then it's doubtful if they'd make any sense."

The box drew itself up to its full two inches and replied in a deep resonant voice. "I'm not one of your run of the mill twentieth century matchboxes. I'm not just a drawer full of wood splinters with red noses and a one-line joke printed on my back. I am Omni, the omniscient micro computer."

"Oh, I see," Oswald lied, trying to sound well informed and completely at ease with the novel idea of having an intelligent conversation with a know-all computerised matchbox.

"I belong to John Buttadaeus, the human time traveller from the twenty sixth century. We came here together from the future. I am his loyal and trusted helper."

Oswald raised his eyebrows sceptically.

"I will prove it, if you like. I could answer all the questions you have been asking yourself."

The Wizard dropped his book on the desk, flopped down in an armchair and stared at the talking matchbox thoughtfully. Somehow this computer must have been left behind when its master took off with Malcolm. This unexpected offer of help sounded like an offer he couldn't refuse. But he had one reservation. Why would the box turn on its master, just to help him?

Omni waited, alert and buzzing in a low tone, its light flashing like a doll's house jukebox. Oswald took his time considering the situation. Tired of waiting, the box spoke again.

"It is obvious John Buttadaeus must have gone into the past. If he took your brother into the future, Malcolm would cease to exist and then he would be unable to help my master. Man cannot travel into his own future, only into his past."

"Pull the other leg! That can't be true. What about John Whatshisname? He's a man isn't he? And you just told me you travelled with him from the future."

"My master, John Buttadaeus, can travel in time as far as the twenty sixth century because that would be going forward into his own past. Your brother lives in the twentieth century; anything happening after today is his future. Take it from me, if he ventures into his own future he will just vanish. He'll cease to exist."

Oswald nodded slowly; now he was beginning to understand.

"What about you? Does that apply to computers as well?"

"I travel only as a passenger with my master. I am bound by the same restrictions as he. My memory banks contain only what has happened up to the day we left the twenty sixth century on our time travels."

"Does that mean you know my future?" Oswald asked eagerly, sitting forward on the edge of his chair. A sudden thought had struck him; maybe he was destined to figure prominently in the years to come, perhaps as a world renown High Wizard or something equally grand.

"I will know about you only if you become famous; if you win the lottery, murder someone, or somehow get mentioned by the media.

I'm only an information storing device not a fortune teller...that appears to be more in your line, as you're a High Wizard."

Oswald took heart at this last comment. The box certainly knew a lot about him. It knew he was a High Wizard, for a start. Sill harbouring dreams of future fame; he speculated on the possibilities. Maybe he would become court astrologer or fortune teller by appointment to the King, later in his life.

"What makes you say that, Omni? Will I become a latter-day Nostradamus or get very rich, writing the astrology pages in a Sunday supplement?" Oswald asked, possibilities of future riches filling his head.

"All I know of you I learned when I attended your lecture on the Rule of Inevitability."

"Oh! Is that all?" Bitter disappointment showed in the wizard's voice.

Omni tried to soften the blow, recognising the dejected tone in Oswald's voice.

"Don't despair. Your Rule is partly correct. It's a small part of a much bigger truth."

Oswald grimaced. A small part was not enough for his overblown ego, he craved a leading role.

Omni tried again. "If I understand you correctly, your Rule states that things achieved by magic have a habit of reversing themselves by putting themselves right as time goes by. As far as it goes, you are on the right lines. What you have noticed is part of a much larger picture, which students of the occult will come to understand fully during the next two hundred years."

The High Wizard digested this information. He was surprised to hear that wizards like himself would still be practising their spells two hundred years into the future. He was really quite flattered that it would take them so long to improve on his Rule.

"What exactly will they discover?"

178

"If I told you that, I would be breaking the golden rule of time travel. It is forbidden to alter the past as this will interfere with the future."

"But that's just what your bloody master is doing by kidnapping my brother!" Oswald snorted.

"I know." Omni sighed deeply. "That's why I decided to break my silence and talk to you in the first place."

Oswald was about to ask more questions, when they were interrupted by an urgent knocking on the street door.

"Good God! It's the police!" He dived under the table. In his panic he completely forgot he could make himself invisible to human eyes long before they could climb the stairs to his hideout.

"Police! Whatever have you done?" Omni enquired.

"I was given some forged ten pound notes by your boss. The idiot made a good job of them but he used the same number on every single note! The police think I made them."

Omni considered this news but didn't comment on it.

The hammering on the street door sounded even louder and a deep male voice shouted through the letterbox.

"I'm sure you're in there, Mr Gotobed. I'm not going away until you let me in."

Oswald turned deathly pale, the law had found his hiding place. He would be charged with escaping arrest and imprisoning a police officer. They'd surely clap him in handcuffs this time and chain him to the cell wall. They might even resort to the ancient stocks in the police station yard. No amount of going invisible would get him out of that. There would be no way he could help Malcolm then. He and his brother were both done for.

Chapter Thirty Four

The hammering on the front door began again. Oswald tucked himself under the library desk. Omni checked his sensors for life forms in the street.

"It's that large man in the onion bag vest who first borrowed the time machine."

"Oh, you mean Frank Hogg, the clock restorer." Oswald sighed with relief. The street door took another battering. This time the shouting was even louder. Oswald listened carefully, confirming for himself that it was indeed Frank's voice.

"I'd better let him in before the neighbours call the police. If the law turn up I'm finished and I won't be able to help my brother."

"Would it not be wise to go invisible again? What if someone passing by sees you at the door?" Omni shouted, as the Wizard made his way down the stairs.

The bolts shot across and the door swung open.

"Come in quickly Frank and close the door after you." Oswald's disembodied voice ordered the clock restorer into the hallway.

Frank scratched his head in disbelief. The door had just spoken to him in Oswald's voice. Must be some kind of personal intercom, like they had in them posh flats overlooking the market square.

"I'm in now. Shall I come up stairs?" Frank shouted loudly from the hallway.

"Please yourself, Frank. But there's no need to shout," Oswald's voice spoke quietly, from just behind the big man's back.

Frank whipped round, wondering how he had missed seeing the Druggist. The big man was shocked to find nobody was there.

"How did you do that, Mr Gotobed? Your voice came from just behind my neck. I'd swear you were actually here."

"I am here, you idiot. Get up the stairs." Oswald dug his fingers into Frank's broad back and pushed him towards the first step.

The clock restorer reluctantly climbed the stairs to the library. He knew Oswald Gotobed was High Wizard to the RUFS; that much was common knowledge among the locals. He'd even heard a few peculiar rumours about the man, but this was his first experience of his magical powers.

"Sit down and tell us what you want, Frank," the disembodied voice suggested.

"Who's us? Are there several of you? What are you, aliens or ghosts?" Frank was getting very nervous. He thought he recognised the voice but as far as he could see, there was no one in the room with him.

"He means me," the black matchbox explained.

Frank gulped, rubbed his eyes and stared at the small paperweight. He reminded himself he was stone cold sober and pinched his leg to check that he was awake.

Oswald reversed the invisibility spell, slowly regaining solid shape, reappearing in front of the bookshelves. Frank watched with eyes like saucers, as the Wizard grew from a faint smoke-like image into his normal chubby self, finally solidifying and blotting out the rows of books immediately behind him.

"Now, what exactly is so damned important? You nearly knocked the door down."

Frank had temporarily forgotten his mission to use the time machine. The strange events since his arrival had completely driven his own problems out of his mind. With a start he remembered why he had come.

"Oh yes! I need to borrow the time machine, Mr Oswald."

"Don't we all! If I knew where it was, you could have the damn thing!"

"It is imperative we get my master to return." Omni's metallic voice broke into the conversation.

"Who's he? Is this some kind of joke or are you throwing your voice?" Frank mouthed the question nervously at the Wizard.

"That's Omni. Omni meet Frank Hogg, clock restorer and Hell's Angel. Frank meet Omni, all knowing, all singing, all dancing matchbox!" There was just a hint of sarcasm and desperation in Oswald's voice.

Omni ignored the new arrival and spoke urgently to the Wizard. "We need to formulate plans before it is too late. What I have learned since I met you, Oswald Gotobed, means my master is in grave danger if anything should befall your twin brother."

" Too right, he is! He'll be in even graver danger when I get hold of him," Oswald scowled.

Frank wriggled uncomfortably in his chair. He was not as adaptable as the Wizard. He needed more time to come to terms with small, talking boxes. Frank had always lead a sheltered life where electronic gadgets were concerned. At home Freda always set the video recorder for him and he never used an electric razor.

Oswald noticed Frank's uneasiness. Foreseeing problems, he tried to think of a way to divert the big man's attention.

"Be a good chap and nip across to the chippy and get me some breakfast, please Frank." He handed over a five-pound note. "Better get yourself some too, but please don't mention my name to anyone you meet. Now..."

Frank needed no second bidding, he was out of the chair and down the stairs before Oswald had completed the second sentence.

"....make sure you shut the door after you." Oswald shouted after him. But Frank moved like the wind when food beckoned and the warning did not catch up with him.

Chapter Thirty Five

The only trouble with Frank Hogg was his appetite. The thought of food drove everything else out of his mind. With the smell of frying cod enticing him over to the chip shop he forgot to close the door to the Union building on his way out.

Sergeant Peele had searched all over Runford for the escaped Druggist. He had sent men to the High Street pharmacy, questioning Roger and the locum pharmacist. There he learned that both Gotobed brothers had mysteriously disappeared. A police posse called on Lydia at the Dog in a Doublet and in spite of spending heavily on several rounds of drinks, learned nothing new about the Druggist from her or the regulars.

Theo Willis, one of the Druggist's known associates, was unable to help them, but he did suggest they try the RUFS' library again, as Oswald often did his research there.

"It is imperative that we get my master to return. He is in grave danger." Omni was repeating its dire warning when they were interrupted by the arrival of police.

"Allo, 'allo, 'allo. Anyone in?" The sergeant's deep voice echoed up the stairway to the Union library.

184

Oswald did not hear the policeman at first. He was too engrossed in his conversation with Omni. The box however, with its supersensitive artificial ears, heard every sound.

"Shush! I heard someone calling."

Oswald stopped and listened.

"Mr Gotobed? Is anyone there?" The questions came again.

"Good God! That really is the police! Who let them in?" The Wizard panicked. His first thought was to get out of the library and the only way open to him was up into the attic.

Sergeant Peele clomped up the stairs from the street, a constable dutifully following behind him. The officer pushed open the door to the book room just as Oswald reached the top step of the iron staircase and slipped out of sight.

"The room's empty, constable. I could have sworn I heard voices up here." Peele took stock of his surroundings, noted the books and papers strewn about the table, applied the rules of detection he had learned at Police College and deduced someone had been there very recently.

"Funny about those voices. Someone must have been up here when we arrived." The policeman walked in the direction of the iron staircase.

Omni, who needed Oswald's help as much as the Druggist needed its, decided to create a diversion. A high pitched whistle emitted from the small black paperweight, then it did a passable imitation of a radio, repeating some of the new items it had come across in its researches.

"This is a news bulletin. Farm prices are falling. The weather looks set to rain and all trains from Euston are delayed by forty-five minutes. The Queen opened parliament today. Arsenal beat Newcastle in the semi-final and snooker was cancelled because of high winds. Jimmy Young reached number one in the hit parade with his recording of..."

"What's that? A transistor radio? That's what we must have heard as we entered the premises."

Omni breathed a sigh of relief. Its subterfuge seemed to be working. Its only problem was keeping up the pretence, it just gathered news and hadn't a clue what normal twentieth century radio programs sounded like. In desperation it turned to music.

"We have a recital of bagpipe music from the town hall." The black box knew it could make a screeching sound and opted for that easy way of hiding its ignorance.

"Can't you turn that thing off, constable?"

"Yes, sir." The policeman picked up the little box, searching for the off knob. Omni clicked its artificial tongue and fell silent.

"Good man. I like listening to bagpipe music but only at a distance. To my mind, Scotland is just about far enough away from South Lincolnshire to appreciate the pipes properly."

Oswald stood on the top step of the spiral staircase, not daring to move, feeling like Don Juan trapped on a lover's balcony. He recovered his senses when Omni began the radio impressions and made good use of the diversion to recite the invisibility spell to himself. He knew he must vanish before the police came up to search the attic.

Frank Hogg returned from the chip shop.

"Oswald. I bought you pie and chips. They were out of sausages," he shouted as he ran up the stairs.

"Hope you don't mind but I got myself a fruit pie with your change because I was feeling peckish." Frank opened the library door and ran straight into the arms of Sergeant Peele of the South Linc's constabulary.

"Carry on Frank. What else were you going to tell Mr Gotobed?" Sgt Peele enquired ominously.

"I...I...I was hoping he was here." Frank lied lamely. If there was one thing the Hell's Angel was bad at, it was subterfuge.

"Sounded to me as if you expected him to be here." Peele's steely grey eyes bore into Frank's open countenance.

Turning back to the constable, he barked. "Search the building. He's here somewhere. I'll guard the door in case he makes a break for freedom."

The young policeman looked everywhere. He moved stools and chairs, lifted up tables and rolled up carpets. He even tipped up the waste paper basket and opened small drawers in his wish to impress his superior, but only when Peele ordered him to check upstairs, did he mount the first step of the spiral staircase.

"There's nothing up there now...the turret clock has gone." Frank spluttered in an agitated voice, trying to divert their attention, for he guessed the Druggist must be up in the attic.

"Eat your lunch before it gets cold." The Sergeant suggested; he was an astute student of human psychology. Frank sat down and unwrapped his chips. In desperation Omni started up the bagpipe music again.

"I thought you had turned that damn thing off?" The sergeant left his position by the door, picked up the noisy box, and shook it violently to dislodge the batteries. Omni had an attack of vertigo and stopped playing.

Oswald, by then completely invisible, felt confident they couldn't catch him and decided to have some fun at the constabulary's expense.

"I'm up here." He shouted from the top of the iron steps, then slid unseen down the banister to the library.

"Let's get him!" Sergeant and constable rushed for the stairs and ran up to the attic.

"Now I'm down here." Oswald chuckled from below them.

They ran back down the spiral stairs to find Frank tucking into his food alone, with no one else in sight.

"Who said that?"

"It wasn't me, whatever it was." Frank exclaimed with his mouth full. Then he had a rare brain wave.

"I think I know what's happening. Mr Gotobed has been practising ventriloquism. He can throw his voice for miles. I was fooled when I came in; I thought he was in the hall downstairs but he was nowhere to be seen."

Sgt Peele grunted in disgust.

"Miles? That means he could be anywhere in Runford. Come on constable we may as well check the pub again."

Oswald waited until he heard them leaving the building and watched them cross the street below the library window before he returned himself to his visible state.

"Now they've gone we can talk in peace, Omni. What did you mean, John Whatshisname is in grave danger? Did you include Malcolm as well, in that comment?"

"I'd better explain myself. When you picked me up from the attic floor you were invisible and I could not detect you in the visible light spectrum so I started a quick DNA analysis of your sweat. You eventually proved visible in my infra red mode because of your body heat, but it was your DNA that was really a revelation to me."

"How come?"

"You have so many genetic traits that match my master, and your twin brother will be practically identical to you. Tell me, do you have any offspring?"

" Me? I'm not even married! Malcolm has a wife but they have no children yet."

"Well, he definitely will have one, later in his life, and that child will definitely figure in my master's family tree."

Oswald frowned as the black box hummed busily. What was this mini computer on about?

"I am searching my memory banks for mention of your family and my master's ancestors. There must be a connection. The DNA never lies."

188

"Ah! I see now. You are saying that my brother's future child will have a family and eventually John Whatshisname will be born into our family. I'm probably the blighter's great, great, great, great, great, great, ever so great, uncle! That's a thought to savour. How can you be so sure I'm not his umpteen times great grandfather?"

"I wasn't sure at first but now I have retrieved the information from my memory store. Your brother will have a daughter about ten months from now. She will figure in my master's bloodline."

Oswald had a sudden flash of understanding.

"I get it now! If your boss kills Malcolm before the daughter is conceived he will have destroyed himself. He can no longer exist in the twenty sixth century because he won't have any ancestors. That's your golden rule of time travel in action. Never tamper with the past, it could drastically alter the future!"

"Precisely." Omni agreed. "Now you see why you and I must combine to help your brother escape."

Frank Hogg screwed up his empty chip paper and was just going to start on the Wizard's packet when he was spotted.

"Hang on a minute, Mr Hogg. Is that my breakfast?"

The restorer grudgingly handed over the food and Oswald sat at the desk and munched the chips, talking to Omni between mouthfuls.

"I must say. I'm fascinated by this glimpse into my brother's future."

"I could tell you some more of the family history, if you promise to forget it as soon as you've heard it." Omni was trying to keep in the Wizard's good books.

"Consider it forgotten already." Oswald grunted between chips, delighted at this chance of a glimpse into his future.

"You will not have any children but some of your brother's descendants will become quite famous.

189

They figure in my memory banks because they were players on the world stage. There is a girl who will win the tennis finals at Wimbledon, a lad who will captain his country's Football team and another female who will become Secretary General of the United Nations."

"Well I never! I never guessed Malcolm had it in him! Must be my side of the family." Oswald felt almost proud to call him brother.

Omni had by this time grown to trust the Wizard.

"I suppose I could give you a hint about your Rule of Inevitability. It may save you a lot of trouble in the future."

Oswald sat forward on the edge of his chair and nodded vigorously. This was more like it. What was the good of hinting at things and not telling him properly. He never could stand being teased.

"Do you understand the basic rules of algebra? Do you remember learning that two pluses make a positive? That two negatives can make a plus but two unlike signs always make a minus?"

Oswald screwed up his face in disgust. What was the stupid matchbox getting at? Why quote schoolboy maths he had gladly forgotten?

Frank picked his teeth, ignoring the conversation completely. If it wasn't about food, clocks or motorbikes he wasn't interested.

"In Time Magic lore, two rights make a right. A right and a wrong never make a right." Omni recited the saying in a singsong, robot voice. "If you do the right thing for the wrong reason or the wrong thing for the right reason, it will not work out. When you cast a time spell for your own ends it will always reverse, either immediately or at some future date."

"Ah! I think I see what you're getting at. If I cast an unselfish spell to help other people it will work, and stay working. If I do it for my own interests it will go wrong."

190

Oswald scratched his head. "I suppose it's some kind of natural justice. What about my weather magic? That's nothing to do with time, is it? And when I made fine weather for the town garden fete, it was not for selfish reasons, but it still rained later in the year to make the rainfall figures average."

"Correct me if I'm wrong, but I'm sure you wanted fine weather at a particular time. That could be classed as time magic. And I bet you charged a fee for the services."

Oswald scowled to himself. This clever box knew too much about his motives.

"So, what about the fruit pie and the beer?"

"You must have been reversing the spell so that you could consume the items yourself."

"I see. If I had intended giving the fruit pie and the pint of ale to Frank here, you are saying it would have worked?"

"I've had one but I'd love another." Frank beamed; he had instantly tuned into their conversation at the mention of food.

"Exactly." Omni answered Oswald; they both ignored the restorer.

"What's the good of being a Wizard if you can't conjure things up for your own use?" Oswald whined. Doing good deeds for the sake of it was more Malcolm's style than his.

"Enough of this," Omni said briskly. "Have you recharged your calorie store? Can we get on with rescuing your brother now?"

Chapter Thirty Six

"What if I entice my master back here? When he realises where he has left me, he will come to collect me." Omni suggested to Oswald.

"How are you going to contact him to tell him where you are?"

"He can pick up my emergency signal anywhere in time and space. He will be able to home in on it. Then you must delay him long enough for me to explain about his ancestors."

"Detain him? Sounds a bit physical to me," Oswald exclaimed doubtfully. "This could well be a job for a bigger man; someone like Frank Hogg."

Frank, who was munching on the cold remainders of Oswald's chips and oblivious to what was being planned, nodded happily at this mention of his name.

When lunch break was over Oswald took Omni back to the attic and replaced him on the floor, exactly where he had found him. Frank followed them up the spiral staircase. He wanted to check with his own eyes, that the turret clock was no longer there.

"We are going to entice the clock back again, Frank. When it arrives it will have my brother and that chap in an aluminium suit sitting on it. I want you to ambush the old man and stop him using those brass levers. Then Omni will have a word with him and that should sort everything out."

"Does your promise to sort everything out, include my problems with Freda?"

"Don't tell me you've still not got her back home, Frank. By now I thought she would have seen sense."

Frank shook his head sadly and looked as if he would burst into tears. He had tried all his friends for suggestions but nothing seemed to have worked.

"I'll try some magic later and get her to come home to you, but only if you help me and Omni." Oswald was ready to promise anything.

The black matchbox started transmitting its homing signal once more, emitting a single beep every few seconds as it had when Oswald discovered it. Frank hid in the darkest corner of the room, crouched down low, ready to spring onto the clock when it returned. Oswald stood at the top of the stairs and prayed.

Thirty minutes of beeping passed slowly. On the surface nothing appeared to be happening. The two men grew restless; Frank's stomach even started rumbling again. Omni put its homing signal on to automatic mode and took a nap to conserve energy.

Suddenly, from far off, there came the sound of a tram pulling into the depot. With a whoosh, the turret clock appeared. At first it wavered like some mirage in a blazing hot desert then it stabilised and popped into sharp focus. Oswald was disappointed to see a lone metal clad figure seated at the controls. There was no sign of his brother!

John Buttadaeus looked around the attic, saw the red light flashing on Omni and rose from his seat to retrieve his lost computer. Frank Hogg lumbered into action.

It was a brief struggle. The Hell's Angel tried to get an arm lock on the old man but he was far too slow. Frank missed his quarry and fell across the turret clock, knocking all the wind out of himself. John Buttadaeus leaned over and pressed the back of his assailant's neck. Frank blacked out, rolled off the clockworks and thudded onto the attic floorboards, as limp as a wet newspaper.

The time traveller brushed himself down and made to get off the machine again to reach out for Omni, but he was too late.

When Frank collapsed over the clock frame, the brass Time lever became entangled in his string vest again, this time it broke away from the machine. The clock restorer was no lightweight and his whole bulk had landed on the small projection. The time machine was nudged into action by the impact and John Buttadaeus, helpless to reverse the effect, started to go transparent as he was whisked away into the depths of time.

"Not so bloody fast, John Whatsyourname!"
Already semitransparent, John turned at the sound of Oswald's voice and stared open mouthed in astonishment.

"I just left you in the 14th century. How did you get back here..?" His voice trailed away into the distance as he vanished completely.

"You kidnapped my brother. I want him back again." Oswald shouted after the apparition, making a magic pass at the old man to cast an immobilising spell. Sparks shot from the Wizard's fingers. Blue lights danced all over the fading image of the metal suit like lightning on a copper conductor, but it was no use. As inevitably as a loose boat on a turning tide, the turret clock and its reluctant passenger slipped away.

"Damn! I've lost my brother and now my only link to him has done a bunk." Oswald picked up Omni and went over to help Big Frank, who was lying unconscious on the attic floor.

"Damn that stupid time traveller!" Oswald swore to himself. Now he had really messed it up. Malcolm was somewhere in the 14th century and John Whatshisname had escaped into the time/space continuum, to heavens knows what date and place. It was all a bloody mess.

"Come on Frank. Stop playing dead." The Wizard cast a simple reviving spell and woke the big man out of his trance.

"Did I get him?"

194

"No chance. He's vanished into the maze of time again like a ferret down a rabbit hole. Come down to the library. We must think what to do next."

"Hang on a minute, I've got something hard stuck in me vest." Frank disentangled the brass lever from his clothing and held it up for the Wizard to see.

"Oh dear! That means John Whatshisname has hurtled off on his clock without one of his controls. Even if he wants to come back he can't. He's stuck! What a bloody disaster!"

"I didn't do it on purpose, Mr Gotobed," Frank apologised.

"It's no good standing here like two drunks who've missed the last bus home. Let's go down to the library and give this situation some serious thought." Oswald led the way down the spiral staircase and slumped into an armchair, where he sat with his head buried in his hands. It was a real problem. If John Buttadaeus was to be believed, Malcolm was lost somewhere in the 14th century. Oswald felt as helpless as a child's balloon in a force ten gale.

Chapter Thirty Seven

Still virtually a prisoner in the RUFS library, Oswald spent his time searching the History books as well as the Magic sections of the book collection. The only clue he had to Malcolm's whereabouts was that chance mention of the 14th century. The problem was, he hadn't a clue where he could be. Was he back in medieval Europe, lost in Timbuktu, or was he still in Runford?

"Frank, I'll have to rely on you to keep me fed and supplied with drinks. I daren't show my face to any one else in case Sergeant Peele hears about it. If you'll help me, I'll try and sort out your problems with your wife. But first I must rescue Malcolm. It could be a matter of life or death."

"I'll keep fetching the chips and beer if you keep paying for them, Mr Gotobed. And I'll be very grateful if you could find the time to work some of your magic on Freda."

The Wizard nodded absentmindedly from the top of the library steps. He had reached the last of the local history books and was reading an account of Runford priory in the plague years of 1349 and 1350.

"God Lord! It say's here the priory of Runford was saved from the pestilence by the intervention of God's right hand man. Saint Malcolm arrived from nowhere and helped nurse the monks back to health. He set up a hospital and taught them all manner of secrets to combat the plague before he vanished as quickly as he had arrived." Oswald slammed the volume shut and waved his fist triumphantly in the air.

"That's my brother. Always helping others. He seems to have got himself canonised into the bargain, but that's no surprise to me, either."

Frank looked up from the armchair where he was reading the local paper and grinned sheepishly at the Wizard.

He had no idea what the old chap was going on about but it was a relief to see him smile again.

"Does that mean you can bring back Freda for me?"

"All in good time. Here, go and fetch some fish and chips for both of us." Oswald tossed some pound coins down to his helper and slid down the rail of the wooden library steps, the history book still open in his hands. Frank had departed before the Wizard's feet touched the floor.

After their meal Frank decide to go home. He had several clocks to repair and his tea to think about.

Oswald was relieved to see him go, the constant rumbling of his stomach was most off putting, when he was trying to do some research. Frank promised to call early next morning to bring Oswald's breakfast. The Wizard, certain that he had located his lost brother in the depths of the 14th century, conferred with Omni.

"You haven't said a word since your master left in such a hurry, Omni. What do you think, my old matchbox? Is this Saint Malcolm my twin brother?"

Omni emitted a high pitched whirr as it checked its memory banks. At last it spoke.

"Yes. There seems no other logical explanation. This medieval healer is reputed to have used medical knowledge centuries ahead of his time. I think we can assume he's your man. I have been engrossed in plotting the space/time co-ordinates of the time machine during the last few days and it certainly travelled to Runford in the winter of 1349. It arrived there on Christmas Eve."

"Marvellous! That confirms it." Oswald chuckled with delight. "Now all I have to do is find a way of conjuring myself back to that time and bring Malcolm back with me."

"Beware the selfish use of time magic." Omni warned.

"Mind your own business. I will rescue my brother if I must die in the attempt!"

197

The black box fell silent, its brief did not include prophecies. It continued trying to locate its master who was stranded somewhere in the network of time because of the damage to the turret clock.

Oswald went to the index of volumes on Time Magic and thumbed through the entries on advanced spells. Making an individual fruit pie travel back a few hours was child's play compared with what he was going to attempt. He searched and made notes into the small hours of the morning, using up every one of the emergency candles in the process.

Eventually, nearing first light, he perfected the obscure spell he needed.

"Recite the Latin words, concentrate your whole consciousness on the mind picture and make the magic passes with both hands. Oh yes! I almost forgot. And hold your breath! I hope the centuries pass by quickly. I could hold my breath for a long time when I was a lad and used to dive and swim regularly in the river, but now I'm not that fit!" Oswald muttered to himself as he worked out his strategy.

"How am I going to know when I arrive at Christmas 1349? You got any good ideas, Omni?

The black box sighed deeply at this tiresome interruption to its calculations, but it understood how illogical humans could become when they locked onto an idea.

"Don't you have a perpetual calendar? Something that moves on each new day?"

"Perpetual calendar? We've got one at the shop to show the customers what date to write on the back of their prescriptions, but no way does it go back six hundred years! There wasn't even a National Health Service in those days."

"You can make adjustments to cover the time span and to allow for the changes in the calculation of dates. Bear in mind, there have been many changes to the calendar, like the adjustment of ten days that Pope Gregory instigated in 1582," Omni suggested helpfully.

"Oh hell! How the devil can I be expected to know all that?"

"Get your perpetual calendar, if you must go ahead with this ridiculous idea. I suppose I can calculate the necessary adjustments." The box sighed again. It had a lot on its electronic brain and Oswald was interrupting it too often.

"You work out the dates. I won't be long." Oswald made himself invisible again, left the security of the library and crossed the dark deserted High Street to the chemist shop. At that early hour there was no one about, only a gang of cats raiding the fish shop dustbins, looking for discarded fish bits. These animals scattered, hissing and spitting when Oswald passed by. They couldn't see the Wizard but they sensed he was there.

Inside the dispensary, the Druggist left a brief note for the locum pharmacist, telling him to continue running the shop until further notice, then he took the perpetual calendar from its nail above the counter and hurried back to the library.

For the next two hours the Wizard worked under Omni's guidance to set up his timeometer. Finally, everything was ready for his attempt to put back the clock.

Chapter Thirty Eight

"Are you coming with me to the 14th century?" Oswald asked Omni, hopefully.

"No. I need to be here in case my master returns."

"Oh! Are you expecting him? How come he can still travel about in time without that brass lever?"

"I have pinpointed the turret clock's time co ordinates. Eventually it will reappear in the attic above us, when real time catches up with it. I only hope my master has the good sense to stay on the clock frame and not wander off."

"Wish me luck." Oswald stood in the centre of the library carpet and started reciting his spell.

"Wait! Are you mad? Don't do it here," Omni yelled in a high pitched voice.

"What? What's the matter now?"

"I would go downstairs to the ground floor if I were you. When you travel back to the days before this building existed you might fall through the floor and break your leg."

Oswald frowned. He hadn't thought of that possibility, but it was obvious really, for the Union building was early Victorian and he would be going back a lot further than that. Time travel was more complicated than he had anticipated.

He marched down the stairs and went out into the enclosed back yard behind the Union building. There he prepared to depart once more. He recited the Latin words, his hands wove the magic passes. He held his breath and gave it his all, remembering to keep one eye on his timeometer.

The Union building vanished in a blur, cobbles replaced the metalled roads. The cars vanished, and horses increased in popularity. Cobbled streets became dirt tracks. Green fields replaced the houses and streets. The town shrank to a huddle of thatched hovels sheltering under the stone walls of a vast, churchlike building. That must be Runford Priory before it was destroyed by Henry the Eighth, Oswald thought hopefully.

He checked his calendar and saw the year was 1400. He was almost there! He slowed down his incantations and then made his first mistake; he started thinking about taking a second gulp of air.

With the years ticking by Oswald fought to hold his breath, but it was too much for him. He was like a skin diver trying to reach the bottom of a deep pool. Each extra inch deeper put increased pressure on his lungs. He felt as if he would burst with the effort. His face went crimson, his ears popped and the green country scene turned a dull grey. As the year turned back to 1390 he finally panicked. He had a stark choice; to breath in fresh air or lose consciousness. Either way he couldn't win. The Wizard gasped for air, stopped reciting the spell, and was propelled instantly forward to his own time.

"Hell...Hell!" Oswald gasped, collapsing onto the Union yard in the twentieth century. He coughed uncontrollably. It took him ten minutes to recover and get back his breath.

"If I was only thirty years younger! If I hadn't spent so much time in the pub breathing in second hand cigarette smoke. If I'd done more exercise...my old lungs aren't up to such punishment." Then the solution struck him. Oxygen was what he needed; that was what deep sea divers and astronauts relied on.

Gotobed Bros., Chemist and Druggist, supplied medical gases to their asthmatic patients. It would mean another visit to the shop but it would solve his problem.

This time when Oswald stalked invisibly across the High Street the town was awake. The milkman and the paper-boy were weaving their way across the street. Business people were hurrying to catch the early train and the florist was watering her hanging baskets. A stray dog came over and sniffed at his unseen bare feet, then backed away barking furiously, the fur on its neck standing up in terror. He sidled into the shop and pulled the door closed behind him.

The full oxygen cylinders were stored down the cellar, in a room behind the Wizard's workshop. He crept into the storeroom and fitted a valve and mask to a full cylinder. Still invisible, he started to carry the apparatus up the cellar steps, when he was interrupted. Suddenly someone came into the shop above him. The bell rang out as the front door was unlocked and flung open. The locum was a conscientious pharmacist and had caught the early train.

Oswald stood on the stairs, hardly daring to breath. He was invisible but the oxygen cylinder could be clearly seen, balanced on his unseen shoulder. He eased the metal cylinder down onto the wooden steps, not wishing to frighten the locum with the apparition of a flying gas bottle. Unfortunately the wooden stairs creaked under his moving weight.

"Who's there?!" The relief pharmacist called out nervously. Oswald froze and held his breath.

"Is that you, Roger?"

Still no answer.

Cautiously the manager peered down the cellar steps. He saw nothing to explain the sounds he had heard but he did notice the gas cylinder standing on the middle step.

"Whatever was Roger thinking about, leaving that cylinder half way up the stairs? If it fell on someone, it could cause a nasty accident."

The relief chemist was about to go down the stairs to move the obstruction, when the shop door jangled open again and in walked Roger.

"Morning." The trainee's cheerful voice greeted his temporary boss.

"Can you move that oxygen back to the store, Roger. It's dangerous perched on that middle step. I don't know why you left it there in the first place."

Roger frowned and scratched his head. He hadn't a clue why the cylinder was half way up the steps. It certainly hadn't been there when he left for home the previous evening.

202

He scrambled down the stairs and picked it up, intending to carry it back to the store.

"Pst! Roger, its me, Oswald," a disembodied voice hissed in the apprentices ear.

"Mr Oswald!" The lad got no further. The Wizard's unseen hand clamped over his open mouth before he could utter another word.

"I need this cylinder delivering over to the RUFS' building. Put it just inside the front door for me."

The lad took the weighty cylinder in his hands and moved it onto another step.

"Eh up! That's on my bare foot!" Oswald shrieked aloud.

"You alright, lad?" The locum called from the dispensary.

The trainee was an intelligent lad and quick on the uptake. He shouted up to the pharmacist.

"Just trapped my finger but its not serious. I've just remembered. I left this oxygen here to remind me to deliver it first thing this morning."

"Funny place to leave it. You'd better get it to the patient before we open up for business."

"Well done, lad. That was quick thinking. I owe you one," Oswald whispered as he limped up the cellar stairs following in the trainee's footsteps.

Roger crossed the High Street and took the full gas cylinder to the RUFS' library, where he left it just inside the door.

"Thanks again, lad," Oswald breathed into the lad's ear.

The Wizard was better prepared for his second attempt to reach his lost brother in the middle-ages. He stood in the centre of the private yard, took in several deep breaths of Oxygen and recited the time spell yet again. This time the timeometer seemed to turn back at a faster pace and there was still breath left in his lungs when the reading reached January 1350.

Chapter Thirty Nine

January 1350 was a very cold month. England was in the middle of a cycle of freezing winters, which wiped out the vineyards and froze all the rivers and lakes. Oswald shivered uncontrollably as the icy air settled around him and the cold earth froze his bare feet.

The medieval town of Runford was spread out before him in the grip of a terrible winter. Smoke spiralled up from every thatched hovel. The fields lay bare and white. The hedgerows were coated in a sugary confection of hoar frost. Horses and cattle stood in the fields, their breath steaming in the morning air. He reversed the invisibility spell. Dragging the oxygen cylinder with him, he hurried towards the cluster of stone buildings, which he hoped would prove to be the priory.

At the priory gatehouse he was stopped by the gatekeeper, who eyed him up and down in a most suspicious way. Oswald realised he was not dressed for the part and his baggy flannels and tweed jacket did not fit in with 14th century fashions, especially with the temperature several degrees below zero.

The gatekeeper spoke in a broad dialect, reminiscent of a character in Chaucer's Canterbury Tales.

"Halt! Who approaches hither?"

"I am....a...stranger in... these parts." Oswald stammered through his chattering teeth. He was painfully aware that his speech was totally different from the middle English in common use in medieval times. It must have been very obvious he didn't belong there, just by the sound of him. He listened carefully to the guard's reply and realised that the man was keeping all travellers out of the Priory compound because the plague was rife in the area around Runford. Pilgrims and travellers had always been given a night's lodgings at the priory but fear of the Black Death had altered all that.

"Go away," the soldier ordered. "We cannot offer hospitality to travellers at this time. The plague is all around us."

The Druggist wasn't bothered about the infection, he and Malcolm he had been injected against these Typhus type of infections when they went abroad on holiday.

"I know all about that. I am here to see your new healer, Saint Malcolm, or whatever it is you call him."

The man frowned at the unfamiliar accent but caught the mention of Malcolm's name. He leaned towards the traveller, staring intently into his face, then smiled in recognition.

"I'm sorry, Brother Malcolm. Forgive me. I didn't recognise you out of your monk's habit." He stepped aside and let the time traveller into the priory yard.

Oswald realising he had been mistaken for his twin brother, tried to act nonchalantly and walked towards the nearest building, pretending he knew where he was going. From the guard's reaction he had come to the right place and at the right time because Malcolm was already known there.

The priory infirmary was busy. Several of the brothers had gone down with the plague, which had spread like a fire through the area, for no one realised the disease was caused by the lack of proper drains and sanitation. Oswald faltered on the flagstone floor, his feet were numb with cold and bleeding from cuts he had suffered walking barefoot over the stony fields.

"Come, brother. I will wash your feet as the disciples washed our Lord's. You have no need to do such penance. You should use stout footwear when you leave the Priory to gather herbs from the hedgerows." An elderly monk took Oswald by the arm and guided him into the hospital. The Druggist meekly allowed himself to be led into the stone building and sat down before a huge log fire. Warm water was fetched from the kitchens, a mixture of dried herbs was stirred into it and his frozen feet were plunged into the bowl. His toes tingled and the cuts stung as feeling returned to his numbed limbs. The aromatic odour of the medicinal herbs rose around him as he sat huddled in front of the spitting logs. Gradually Oswald thawed out.

"It's the least I can do, Brother Malcolm. It is small payment for the unceasing help you have given the other sick brothers." The kindly monk handed Oswald a mug of hot broth from a caldron suspended over the fire and draped a coarse brown robe over his hunched shoulders.

The Wizard drank the salty herring broth and felt the warmth trickle down inside him. Slowly he returned to normal. Realising, he still had the oxygen cylinder at his side, he pulled it closer to him, draping his robe over it to hide it.

"God! What wouldn't I give for some twentieth century medicines." That prayer reached Oswald's ears from an adjoining room. Instantly he recognised his brother's voice.

"Malcolm!" The Wizard rose from his seat and rushed towards the familiar tones.

Not for years had Oswald greeted his brother with such enthusiasm. He flung his arms around his twin's shoulders and sobbed his name again. All the ill feeling and rivalry was forgotten. The Gotobed brothers were united in their joy at finding each other alive in such an unlikely place. Like siblings the world over they would argue and fight but when one of them was in danger their true feelings came out.

206

"Oswald! I am pleased to see you. How in the name of God did you get here?"

"By travelling through time. The same as you."

"Is that how I got here?" Malcolm was wide eyed at this information. "I was beginning to think I belonged in this century and I had some sort of madness upon me. The memories of my past life seemed like hallucinations but my medical training is real enough and it is proving invaluable to these poor sick souls."

Oswald noticed that Malcolm was already beginning to speak like one of the locals.

"You're not mad, brother. You were kidnapped by John Buttadaeus, the time traveller, and left in this time period as a hostage. You are still in Runford but this is the 14th century."

"Yes, I know I'm still in Runford. I took a walk to where our chemist shop should have been and found it was a swineherd's cottage."

"I always said it resembled a pigsty." Oswald quipped.

"These unfortunate people are suffering from the plague. They think it is God's will that I have been sent to help them. With my pharmaceutical knowledge I have been able to make a vast difference. Even elementary hygiene and nursing skills are lacking here. I could do more if only I had some of our modern medicines with me."

"I've come to take you back, Malcolm." Oswald explained why he had ventured so far back in time and that he was in a hurry to return to his own century. He was already missing his creature comforts and he knew that he must be ready when John Buttadaeus reappeared in the Union attic. As they spoke, he adjusted his robe, accidentally uncovering the metal cylinder he was carrying.

"Is that oxygen? Marvellous! We have several cases of pneumonia in the hospital. It will make all the difference to them."

"Now you hang on a minute. This gas is essential to us if we are ever to return to our own time."

"Surely you wouldn't deny a sick man a slim chance of life?"

Put like that, Oswald knew he had little choice. He handed over the cylinder and helped his brother set it up at a patient's bedside.

Chapter Forty

The same morning that Oswald travelled back to the fourteenth century, Frank Hogg arrived at the Union building with some cold toast he had made for the Wizard's breakfast. He parked his motorbike at the kerb and took the food upstairs to the library.

"Mr Gotobed. Yoohoo, Mr Gotobed, where are you?"

"He's gone." Omni explained.

Frank was still not comfortable holding a conversation with a small black box but he took a deep breath and asked.

"Gone where?"

"Back in time to rescue his brother."

"Oh well, there's nothing for me to do here then. Do you mind if I eat his toast then go home and get on with some work?"

"Go by all means. I will contact you if you are needed."

Frank shuffled his feet and considered this offer. How could Omni get in touch with him? It could hardly catch a bus to his workshop. It hadn't any legs for walking, and it certainly couldn't ride a motorbike!

"I can easily hack into your primitive telephone system. Wait for my phone call." Omni had guessed what the restorer was thinking.

All the way home, Big Frank thought about his missing wife. Moodily he drove along the centre of the main road, bumping down hard on each set of cat's eyes, imagining each one was that woman, Gabby. He felt no joy at returning home. There would be an empty house with a lonely unmade bed, a bare refrigerator and several days of unwashed pots waiting on the table.

"That bloody woman has a lot to answer for," he growled into his helmet as he leaned viciously on his handlebars, forcing the front wheel down heavily onto the last of the cat's eyes that dared peer up from their hole in the tarmac.

Frank was in for a surprise when he arrived home. The kitchen table was spotlessly clean and all traces of his recent meals had been swept away. There was a vase of flowers placed in the centre of a clean tablecloth and a bowl of fruit sitting invitingly beside it. Further examination showed the whole room had been tidied. The empty beer cans had gone, the greasy fingerprints and traces of pork scratchings had been wiped from the TV screen. Screwed up crisp packets no longer littered the settee and the cushions had been plumped up invitingly.

"Is that you, Frank?" A light female voice called from the bedroom.

He raced up the stairs, two steps at a time. By some miracle he just knew that Freda was back. Oswald Gotobed had kept his word. Frank flung open the bedroom door and charged inside, his brawny arms open wide to welcome her home.

"My love..." He faltered as he recognised the plump young figure spread out on the bed.

"Whatever are you doing here, Samantha?" The vision of his wife's shapely body changed to the reality of plump Samantha, the Hell's Angel with the tight blonde curls glued to her head. She was stretched out naked on his bed.

Frank was so taken aback he did not hear the back door open or the light footsteps cross the kitchen as another caller hesitated on the threshhold, then tiptoed to the bottom of the stairs.

Samantha explained her presence.

"I've cleaned up everywhere. You need a woman. I've decided you need looking after Frank Hogg. If that stupid Freda can't be bothered to do it, I will."

Frank took a step back, shocked at the wanton display of bare flesh. She was completely naked. He could even see the lines where the seams on her tight leather jeans had dug into her bottom. He held his hands up to cut out the vision and looked away in acute embarrassment. She was a nice kid but she'd got the wrong idea.

"I saw how you bought those chocolates for her. I followed you when you rode into town like some knight on your charger to get her back. I saw a million quid go up in smoke when she refused your present. She doesn't deserve you, Frank. I'll move in and make you happy." Samantha smiled invitingly, parting her red lips to show the steel brace on her front teeth. Rising quickly from the bed, the teenage siren wrapped her arms around him, pressing her bare breasts against his string vest, pushing him back against the bedroom door, which closed firmly behind him, cutting off his retreat.

Frank was nonplussed. He had hoped Freda had returned to him but too late he realised his mistake. This young girl had decided to move in on him. Most of the lads would have torn off their leathers and joined her between the sheets but he had thoughts only for his absent wife.

Samantha pressed home her advantage and pulled him towards her, pressing her firm nipples into his chest.

"Yoohoo, Frank. Are you up there in the bedroom?" A familiar female voice called from the kitchen below them.

"Good God! That's Freda's voice! It really is her this time!"

Frank almost fainted in fright. He disentangled himself from the bare limbs draped about him and panicked.

"What am I going to do? She's come back and she'll find me in the bedroom with another woman. Oh my God! Hide yourself Samantha. Put some clothes on. Hold your helmet over your whatnot. Get under the bed. Do something!"

Samantha grinned triumphantly and lay back on the sheets, parting her legs invitingly and pouting seductively at him. If they were to be caught in the act she would make the most of her opportunity. She was a big girl and she certainly wasn't afraid of Freda Hogg.

Freda slowly climbed the stairs, her footsteps creaking ominously on each successive step. Frank lost his bottle and tried to open the sash window, intending to leap into the yard like a stunt cowboy, hoping to land astride his motorbike saddle and make his escape. Freda pushed open the bedroom door and peeped into the room.

The sash window refused to open. Frank had forgotten; he had nailed it shut in the winter when the draughts had caused a problem. He turned like a guilty schoolboy caught apple scrumping and faced his wife. Samantha grinned, opened everything even wider and settled back onto the pillows.

"Get dressed and go home, Samantha. There's a good girl. My husband and I have a lot to discuss." Freda said this in such a mature matter of fact and motherly voice, the young girl did as she was told. Frank stood woodenly in front of the window like a huge Aspidistra, trying to shrink out of sight and numb with anticipation. Any chance of a reconciliation with his beloved Freda must surely have gone out of the window, even though he hadn't.

"Come downstairs, Frank. I've put the kettle on. I've brought some sliced ham for us."

Like a man in a dream, Frank followed his wife down the stairs. She was too calm. There had to be one almighty explosion any second. It was like sitting on a live volcano.

He held his breath, anticipating the backlash, and sat at the table, so frightened he even ignored the food. Finally, unable to stand the suspense, he pleaded.

"What are you going to do, Freda? I know it must have appeared bad to you but it's not as bad as it looks. Please forgive me, Freda."

"I do know what's happened, Frank. I stood listening at the bottom of the stairs for some time before I called out to you. You are a great big kid. Someone's got to look after you and save you from these scheming women."

"Does that mean you're back?" The big man fell on his knees, tears of relief filling his eyes and streaming down his stubble.

"Yes, I've returned. If you'll forgive me and take me back again. I've seen through Gabriella and her tricks. You were no match for her cunning. You were as soft as axle grease in her scheming fingers. She had me fooled for a while, but I eventually saw through her games. She only played up to you to get to me."

Frank stuffed a whole ham sandwich into his mouth and happily slurped his tea. I owe you a big one, Oswald Gotobed, he thought blissfully. Somehow the Wizard had worked a miracle and brought Freda back to him.

Chapter Forty One

Oswald Gotobed sat on his bed in the guest wing of the Priory. He was exhausted. Malcolm and he had spent the whole day visiting the sick in medieval Runford town and tending to the brothers in the hospital.

"Surely you can see, there's nothing to be gained by staying here in the middle ages."

"Oswald, I am a Christian and my duty is to help these people. Look how that oxygen has revived the sick brothers. It is a miracle how you turned up with it."

"It was not a bloody miracle! It was time magic and I came to get you, not to nurse people who died five hundred years before we were born. Don't you see, you are interfering with the natural order of things. You will alter the future and there will be problems."

"Rubbish. If God brought me here, He did it for a purpose."

Oswald looked askance at his brother. Saint Malcolm indeed, he thought resignedly. It wasn't any good pointing out that John Buttadaeus had been responsible for this time warp and he hadn't done it for any altruistic reasons. All the same, he couldn't help admiring his brother's faith.

"Tomorrow we can use the priory kitchens and prepare some herbal medicines. We are both pharmacists and four hands are better than two."

Oswald rolled onto his back and stared up at the smoke stone ceiling. How was he ever going to get Malcolm to see sense?

The twins worked together at their dispensing and prepared a large stock of medicines. They used lard, honey and wine to prepare their ointments, syrups and tinctures from the medicinal herbs gathered in the hedgerows and grown in the Priory gardens. At Malcolm's suggestion some of the novice monks made notes of everything they did and wrote a herbalry for future reference, illustrating the plants with thumbnail coloured sketches and illuminating the capital letters like the artistry in the Book of Kells. Malcolm was in his element; with his knowledge of botany and medicinal plants he planned a complete pharmacopoeia for the brothers and secretly hoped it would finish up in one of the best twentieth century museums.

"We will call it the Runford Pharmacopoeia. In centuries to come they'll marvel at the healing knowledge people had in the 14th century."

Oswald helped him willingly, hoping that the sooner they had completed their task, the sooner Malcolm would come to his senses and agree to go home.

After four weeks of concentrated effort the priory medicine chest was full, most of the sick brothers were showing signs of making a full recovery and the Prior himself had returned from their mother house in France. He asked to see the twins.

"Brother Malcolm, you have worked miracles here. I understand you came under mysterious circumstances but you came in the name of our Lord. Whoever you are we are grateful for your help."

"I think God intended me for this work my Lord Prior. It has been a pleasure and such a contrast from the medical work I am used to."

Certainly more interesting than flogging condoms, aspirins and pig powders, Oswald thought grudgingly.

The Prior eyed Oswald thoughtfully. The monks had reported that Oswald did not attend any of their church services. He seemed totally uninterested in religious matters. There were also rumours that his Latin incantations were not of a religious nature!

"I must thank you as well, Brother Oswald, but I'm not sure in whose name you carry out your healing work."

"In the name of humanity! And I must warn you, we will soon have to be leaving you to continue our journeys."

Malcolm turned and looked askance at his brother. He felt he was doing more good in the 14th century than ever he could in the twentieth century.

Back at their lodgings in the priory guest wing, Oswald brought the subject up once again.

"We had better be off soon, before we do any more harm to the future."

"What harm can there possibly be in healing these sick people?"

"I told you. The first rule of time travel is not to interfere in any way with the past or you will effect the future. Let's say, for the sake of argument, you save a life that would otherwise have ended and that man goes on to have a family…"

"Marvellous." Malcolm interrupted.

"…and that child grows up and starts a war or kills one of your ancestors. You have altered history and in the latter case, we could no longer exist." Oswald nodded emphatically.

"But I'm doing more good here in the 14th century. God must have ordained it."

"Rubbish! John Whatshisname kidnapped you and landed you here. It wasn't love that motivated him, I can assure you."

Malcolm frowned to himself and stroked his chin thoughtfully.

216

Oswald tried again. "What about your wife? Doesn't she deserve to have you back again?"

Malcolm frowned even more and nodded slowly.

Oswald could see he had made his brother think and he decided to play his trump card.

"What about your family?"

"We haven't been blessed with children, you know that."

"I have learned some fascinating things in my time travelling. One of the nicer items to come to my notice is the imminent birth of your daughter."

Malcolm looked shocked then grinned happily to himself.

"That would fulfil all our hopes...you're not just making that up to persuade me to leave, are you?"

"Would I? Anyway it's true. As things stood when I left the twentieth century, you and your dear wife were due to have a baby in ten months time. Of course if you don't return you will start a chain reaction throughout history. Your descendants will not be born and they will not head the United Nations or do the hundred and one other worthwhile jobs they are destined for in the twenty first and twenty second centuries."

Malcolm pursed his lips and stared at this twin brother.

"Honestly, Oswald? Not one of your convenient lies?"

"Straight up, brother."

"Then for my unborn daughter's sake I'll come back with you."

Oswald hugged him tightly and tears of relief ran down his cheeks mingling with the dust on Malcolm's coarse brown habit.

Chapter Forty Two

The Gotobed twin's return journey to Twentieth century Runford was uneventful. In the cold light of the next dawn they left the Priory and made their way to the field where Oswald had first arrived. One of the young monks who was preparing the pharmacopoeia, came with them.

The twins linked hands, each took a deep breath of Oxygen from the little remaining in the cylinder and handed it back to their helper. Oswald set his timeometer and started to recite his Latin spell. Malcolm prayed to himself. There was a sound like the beating of a large bird's wings and the monkish figures vanished into the dawn mist, leaving their young helper believing he had witnessed a miracle.

Minutes later the Gotobed brothers materialised in the Union back yard. Oswald had timed their return to perfection and they arrived back in the twentieth century just ten minutes after he had originally left.

Malcolm opened his eyes and smiled.

"The last four weeks have been a turning point in my life, brother. I will never be the same again. Fancy, I'm to be a father."

"Don't go telling anyone about it," Oswald warned. "Especially your wife; as she hasn't conceived yet!"

"I'm going over to the shop to check everything is running smoothly, then I'll go home." Malcolm strode purposefully out of the yard and across the High Street. Oswald watched the brown-robed figure without a word; it was not his place to remind his brother that he was still dressed like a medieval monk, whose ankles were covered in mud from the trudge across the fields near the medieval Priory.

Malcolm went into the shop and walked up to the counter, where Paddy Murphy was being served by Roger the trainee.

"That's one pound fifty, please."

Paddy handed over a five-pound note and peered along the counter towards the dispensary.

"Is Mr Gotobed in today, lad?"

"No, neither of them."

"What's happened to the pair of them? I heard the police were asking for Oswald, and Lydia tells me Malcolm has taken to wearing fancy dress about the town at night."

"You mean the old scout uniform. I think that was a mistake."

Paddy became aware that someone was waiting behind him. He turned to look at the newcomer and came face to face with a brown clad monk.

"Sorry, Holy Father, to be sure. I didn't mean to keep you waiting."

"What do you mean, Holy Father?" Malcolm muttered, he had completely forgotten he was still dressed in his monk's outfit.

Paddy recognised the voice instantly.

"Good God! It's Malcolm Gotobed, disguised as a scruffy old monk this time. He's turned into one of them transvestites!" The Irishman crossed himself hastily and ran from the shop without waiting for his change.

Roger ushered his embarrassed boss through to the back-shop before any other customers came in.

In the privacy of the RUFS' yard, Oswald made himself invisible again, and went up to the Library, slipping quietly into the room.

"Ah! You're back. You're quite safe for the moment. The police have just left and Frank Hogg has eaten your breakfast and gone home." Omni spoke as soon as the High Wizard entered the book room.

"Of course, you can see me in infra red, I can't fool you, can I."

"I don't need infra red, you forgot to remove your sandals!"

Oswald reversed the spell and made himself visible again.

"Right Omni, down to business. When do we expect your master to come back again? Will it be today or must I stay here until tomorrow?"

Omni hummed like a high-speed gyroscope and checked its data banks.

"This afternoon at one o'clock the turret clock will slip back into our time zone. I cannot predict if my master will be on board but I hope he has had the sense to stay with the machine. By the way, I rang that Hell's Angel with the string vest, as soon as you returned. He's about to knock on the front door again."

Oswald spent the morning planning his reception for John Buttadaeus. He intended to be ready when the one o'clock time machine drew into the attic.

Frank prattled on about his wife returning to him and how indebted he was to the Wizard.

"Well I'm sure you can repay me by helping to trap that bloody time traveller. This time we mustn't let him get the first blow in. Keep your neck away from his immobilising grip and don't break his machine again."

"Ah! That brass lever, Mr Gotobed. I've silver soldered the part that snapped off. All it needs is screwing back onto the clock."

At mid-day Frank fetched fish and chips from the cafe and they ate their lunch. Omni kept checking his calculations and confirming the imminent arrival of the turret clock.

At ten minutes to one, they all went up to the attic and laid their final plans.

"I will stand over here by the top of the stairs and I'll keep Omni in my hand. You must hide by the window on the opposite side of the room. I can distract him while you creep up on him. Whatever you do grab both his wrists first; that way he can't manipulate your neck."

Frank crouched down under the window where the shadows provided excellent cover and they waited for the machine to reappear.

The church clock struck one. The tone reverberated over the town and echoed in the silent attic like a single death knell. There was a faint whirring sound like a humming top approaching and the air moved as the clock frame and its rider began to slip into the present time.

"Welcome back." Oswald shouted to the time traveller. "Glad you could join us again."

Omni let out a high pitched homing signal.

John Buttadaeus turned to see who was speaking and saw the Wizard at the top of the spiral staircase. He furrowed his brow and grimly set his jaw. This reception committee was not welcome.

"I've rescued my brother from the middle ages. You have no hostage to bargain with any more."

John frowned even deeper and looked at his mini computer.

"Is that correct Omni? Has this idiot managed to perfect time travelling?"

"Yes master."

During this exchange, Frank Hogg edged his way towards the aluminium-clad figure. This time he waited until he was almost on top of the man before he leapt forward. He grasped both wrists firmly in his huge hands and pulled John from the machine. "Got ya!"

The big man held the time traveller up like a rag doll, suspending him by his arms with his feet dangling helplessly.

"Don't harm him." Omni shrilled.

"That's right, Frank. Treat him gently but firmly. Bring him down to the library."

John was badly shaken by his treatment at the Hell's Angels hands. When he was sitting unfettered in a leather chair, he scowled and rubbed his sore wrists.

"Now Mr Time Traveller," Oswald shook his finger at the old man. "You and I need to talk."

"And me." Omni chipped in.

"Just explain to me why you came to our era and maybe I can help you."

"I want the secret of the everlasting tomatoes. I am sure I will be able to extract the genetic information and use it to ensure eternal life."

"Tomatoes! What everlasting tomatoes?"

"There was a newspaper report that the winning fruit at last week's vegetable show were everlasting." Omni interrupted.

"Oh Lord!" Oswald laughed aloud. "That's my fault. I told the press that pack of lies."

John Buttadaeus rose from his chair, indignation written all over his face. "I don't believe you! You are only saying this to put me off the scent."

"You have got it wrong. Do you think I would be middle-aged and wrinkly if I could turn the clock back as easily as that? Tell him Omni."

222

"He's right master. I have checked."

The old man sat down heavily and buried his head in his hands. "It's all academic anyway. The time machine is damaged and I have no workshops here to repair it."

Frank pulled the brass lever from his pocket and held it out to the man. "Here. I repaired this for you."

Before Oswald could intervene, John snatched the lever from the restorer's fingers and ran up the stairs to the attic. Desperation lent the old man wings. By the time the Wizard had reached the top step the time traveller was already on his leather seat and inserting the repaired lever. With a whirr like the sound of a lawnmower, clock and passenger dissolved into thin air.

"Which way has he gone, Omni?" Oswald yelled down the stairs.

"He's heading into the past again. Probably going to get your brother in the 14th century before you rescued him."

"Right. This time I won't let him get away."

The Wizard held his breath, recited the time spell and concentrated on catching the time machine. It was a dangerous game, chasing John Buttadaeus into the past. Oswald knew he must intercept the old man before the RUFS' library vanished, or he would fall into the yard below for, unlike the turret clock, he had no space controls. The winds of time roared in Oswald's ears, his eyes watered as he accelerated into the time continuum, hot on the trail of the fleeing turret clock.

In seconds the turret clock came into view. The attic walls were indistinct, the room went rapidly dark and light as nights succeeded days with ever increasing rapidity. The Wizard pointed his fingers at the old man's back and recited an immobilising spell. The clock ground to a halt just as the roof vanished from above their heads. He had stopped the flight just in the nick of time.

Another few days into the past and the Victorian builders would not have erected the Union walls.

"That was too bloody close for comfort." Oswald muttered as he balanced on a new floor joist where the floorboards had not yet been nailed into place.

Oswald teetered like a trainee tightrope walker and staggered across the beam to the turret clock. John Buttadaeus sat motionless like a waxwork figure. The Wizard eased himself onto the seat beside the fugitive and gently pulled back the time lever. Slowly the scene in the attic changed. The roof grew up over their heads, the floorboards clicked into place and the window reappeared in the end wall. As he grew more confident Oswald eased the brass lever towards himself and the time machine returned them both to the present time.

"Frank, come up here and bring Omni with you." Oswald called down to the library as the clock slid to a halt. "I've brought the old man back again and we mustn't lose him this time. Omni, stand by to convince the silly old devil that there's no such thing as everlasting fruit."

They carried John Buttadaeus down to the library, stiff like a statue because Oswald refused to reverse the immobilising spell until he had assurances that the old man would listen to Omni's explanations.

"He can't move but he can hear you, Omni. Go ahead, tell him about the DNA."

The little black box gave a detailed account of how it had discovered the link between Malcolm's daughter and the time traveller. It explained how anything befalling Malcolm would wipe out the whole blood line and the time traveller himself would cease to exist. John listened because he had no choice. He leaned up against the library wall like a grandfather clock, which no one had thought to wind up.

"Honestly there is no secret of eternal life. The only hold you have on the future is to pass on your genes to your descendants, As Malcolm Gotobed will do to you."

Oswald looked over at the old man, trying to gauge his reactions, but the immobilising spell prevented the slightest movement. Not even his eyes flickered in response. He pointed his finger at the old man's head and muttered a few well-chosen Latin phrases. John Buttadaeus sighed deeply and gulped in a mouthful of fresh air.

"Well? Do you believe Omni, now?"

"I suppose so," John grunted, struggling unsuccessfully to move his body, for the spell had only been lifted from his head.

"Tell him about the selfish use of time magic." Oswald prompted.

"He knows," Omni squeaked. "But it shouldn't apply to him. Time machines work on advanced physics, they don't depend on magic spells."

"I see. It's only we Wizards that are bound by the rules of fair play, is it? It strikes me nothing has gone right for Mr Cleverdick here since he tried to alter the past. How do you explain that my omniscient matchbox?"

Omni hummed busily, then cleared its metal throat with a nervous cough.

"I see what you mean, High Wizard. The evidence does appear to point that way. I hadn't realised it until you pointed it out just now."

John turned his eyes on the black box and glared at it darkly. If looks could have destroyed it, the computer would have gone up in smoke.

"For your own good, think about it, Master. Nothing has gone right since you came into the past on this wild goose chase."

"I know, I know!" John burst into tears.

Frank Hogg, who had been listening to all this and not understanding a word of it, took out his grimy handkerchief and dried the old man's cheek for him.

"Don't fret old fellow. Mr Gotobed will sort it all out for you like he did for me and my wife."

Oswald hid his embarrassment by blowing his nose noisily, holding his own handkerchief over his blushes.

"Take him upstairs Frank. Put him on his machine and we will send him forward into the future. I can tell Omni how to reverse the immobilising spell when he's safely on his way."

Frank hoisted the rigid old man onto his shoulder and carried him up the stair, as easily as if he'd been a roll of wallpaper. They seated him at the controls of the time machine and propped the black box up beside him.

"You needn't bother to tell me how to reverse your spell, Oswald. I already know. I've been observing you closely." Omni assured them.

Oswald leaned over the clock frame and pushed the time lever forward. With a noise like a high wind in a tunnel, the turret clock vanished into thin air.

"Do you think that's the last we'll see of him?"

"Hard to say, Frank, but I saw that look of defeat in his eyes when Omni told him the score. I think we've given him the chance to escape with his dignity still intact. He reminds me a bit of Malcolm and myself, but that's not so surprising really, is it."

"If I'm not needed here any more I'll go home to Freda. We have a lot to catch up on." Frank felt he had repaid his debt to the Druggist. "What are you going to do, Mr Gotobed?

"I have an overdue appointment with the Lincolnshire constabulary."

Chapter Forty Three

The police station was quiet when Oswald walked into reception. He stood in front of the desk and held his wrists out to the duty constable, inviting the man to put the handcuffs on him.

The constable ignored the outstretched arms and smiled.

"What can we do for you, Mr Gotobed?"

"I've come to give myself up. Sergeant Peele wants me for passing counterfeit ten-pound notes."

The constable held a whispered consultation with the police woman on the switchboard, then returned to the desk.

"Would you like to sit down for few minutes, sir. I'm sorry to keep you but I'd better go and telephone Sergeant Peele about this."

Oswald was nonplussed. He had been certain that the police would lock him up and lose the key. Surely they had not forgotten his escape from the cells? What about that forgery charge?

Ten minutes later the desk constable returned and came over to him, wringing his hands in a very solicitous manner.

"Sergeant Peele sends his profound apologies, Sir. He hopes there's no hard feelings. He asked me to personally thank you for your help with the Allotment Holders' show. All charges have been dropped against you. You are free to go...Oh! He also said he made a bad mistake giving up his post with the RUFS. He wants to come back as secretary." The officer turned to leave.

"What about that young policeman I locked in the cell?"

"Sergeant Peele hopes you'll forgive him and not press for compensation for wrongful arrest and imprisonment."

"What's happened to the silly old devil to make him change his mind?"

The officer stopped in his tracks and turned to face the Druggist.

"I suppose you'll hear about it soon enough, so I might as well be the one to tell you. He's taken indefinite sick leave. He's sure he's having a nervous breakdown. When he was writing out the report about the forged money he had a vision."

"A vision? What of?"

"He swears a black matchbox appeared on his desk and spoke to him. It told him to drop the charges. All the print vanished off the sample ten-pound notes, leaving blank paper! He hasn't any evidence now." The policeman held up several sheets of white paper and flicked through them.

"Eh up! I saw some writing on one of those sheets." He rifled through the bundle again and located the odd piece. "Well I'll be damned! Look here, it's a message for you, Mr Gotobed."

Oswald took the printed note and read it aloud. "Oswald Gotobed. My master has finally accepted my word that there is no everlasting fruit. We will not be returning to your time. Thank you for your help. Signed: Omni."

"There's some more writing on the back." The policeman exclaimed.

Oswald read the other side

"PS. I know I could find no future references to you in my historical records, but I have a reference to a famous Mrs Oswald Gotobed, a tattooed lady."

"See what I mean?" The constable said. "Sergeant Peele's gone off his head. Even his messages don't make any sense."

"Good old Omni!" Oswald whooped with delight, stuffed the note in his pocket, and ran out of the police station, making straight for the Dog in a Doublet.

228

*If you have enjoyed this book and would like to read
further stories by this author.*

Book one of the Runford Chronicles:

THE FAERIE STONE

Is available from the publisher

*NORMAN COTTAGE
89 West Road
Oakham
Rutland
LE15 6LT UK*

*Check our latest books on our Website.
http://www.users.globalnet.co.uk/~rexm*